TOWER

MEASHA STONE

© Black Heart Publications 2018 All rights Reserved

www.meashastone.com

Black Heart Publications

Editing and Proofreading by Wizards in Publishing

Cover Design by Simply Defined Art

No part of this publication may be reproduced or transmitted in any form or by any means, electronic, or mechanical, including photography, recording, or any information storage and retrieval system without the prior written consent from the publisher and author, except in the instance of quotes for reviews. No part of this book may be uploaded without the permission of the publisher, and author, nor be otherwise circulated in any form of binding or cover other than that in which it is originally published.

This book is a work of fiction. Any resemblance to persons, living or dead, or places, actual events or locales is purely coincidental. The characters and names are products of the author's imagination and used factitiously.

The publisher and author acknowledge the trademark status and trademark ownership of all trademarks, service marks and word marks, mentioned in this book.

ABOUT THE AUTHOR

USA Today Bestselling Author Measha Stone is a lover of all things erotic and fun who writes kinky romantic suspense and dark romance novels. She won the 2018 Golden Flogger award in two categories, Best Advanced BDSM and Best Anthology. She's hit #1 on Amazon in multiple categories in the U.S. and the U.K. When she's not typing away on her computer, she can be found nestled up with a cup of tea and her kindle.

TOWER
EVER AFTER

USA TODAY BESTSELLING AUTHOR
MEASHA STONE

CHAPTER 1

City lights illuminated the street to the point of daylight. Azalea Gothel turned the corner onto Main Street, which would take her to her targeted location. Hood raised to block recognition, she only had a few hours. Any more than that, and she would be found out.

She walked past a narrow storefront selling liquor and cheap thrills, mostly gambling from what the blinking neon lights advertised, and headed to the larger, more sophisticated-looking club. The building stood out from the rest on the strip, towering over all of them, and decorated in a much darker scheme than the rest.

The club resembled a Renaissance mansion, with ominous architecture and two large gargoyles perched on podiums overlooking the entrance. Two towers climbed to a second story with a third rising two stories higher than the others.

The owner had aptly named the club Tower, or maybe he'd built the club around the name.

It didn't matter, and she had much bigger concerns at the moment. Her curiosity had driven her down to the city streets, out of the comfort of her suite where she lived with her mother. But she had only a few hours. If she didn't return home before midnight, her absence would be discovered.

Having an overprotective mother had been annoying growing up. Now, it caused a desperation Azalea had never felt before.

"Hey there, beautiful." A voice from behind her slithered over her shoulder. She quickened her steps. The owner of the voice cursed at her but didn't follow her.

Tower may cater to upscaled clientele, but it brought out the seedy beasts as well. She wasn't completely naïve; she knew better than to think she'd be able to walk the street without at least one man's eyes on her. It was her hair. The golden tresses easily snagged attention.

She pulled her hood closer around her face and came to the entrance of the club. Taking a deep breath, she retrieved her small purse and dug out the cover charge.

"You alone?" The bouncer looked behind her. At such a late hour, the evening was already in full swing, yet there wasn't a line.

"Yes," she said and waved the bills in his direction. "Fifty dollars, right?" She pushed the money at him again when he didn't accept it.

"Take off that coat," he ordered.

She heaved a sigh. She would hardly hide weapons in such a flimsy overcoat, but if it would make the hulking guard take her cash and let her off the street, she'd play along.

Shaking off the garment, she threw it over her arm and thrust the bills at him again. "Okay?"

He looked her over. A smile grew on his lips as his gaze reached her chest, and brightened as it traveled downward.

Snagging the money, he nodded. "Yeah, but if I were you,

I'd stay near the bar and not go wandering around. Less likely to get caught."

She didn't bother to ask him what he meant, since he'd spoken the words directly to her breasts, and made her way in.

Music with low, deep beats played, luring her into the club. She stopped at the coat check to drop her coat and stuffed the ticket into her bag.

As she walked into the main room, the life of the club erupted before her. The music grew more intense, or maybe it felt that way with all the scenes going on around her. The club catered to darker passions, the sort she'd been reading about, fantasizing about. It was how she found the club. Not having much to fill her days outside of her graphic design projects, she delved into every image Google had to offer on the naughty subjects.

Fog swirled across the flooring. She walked toward the bar, remembering what the doorman had told her. She'd get a drink, ease into the ambiance, and then she'd make her rounds. So much to see, so much to take in.

The sharp crack of a whip derailed her mission, and she followed the sound instead. Along the edges of each room, scenes played out. Some were simple—a woman on her knees being petted by the man towering over her—while others were more intricate. A woman hung from the ceiling, wrapped in rope in such a way that she looked more like a piece of art than a sexual plaything. Azalea took a moment to admire the knotting and the design of the rope around the woman's torso and legs before a second snap got her feet moving again.

She made her way through the crowd, feeling men staring at her and hearing a crude murmur, but she paid them no mind. Surveying the room, she realized she was the only woman walking freely about the room without an escort. How had she missed that?

But her vision often became tunneled when she had her mind set. It was one of the flaws her mother had worked hard over the years to relieve her of without any success.

She arrived at the main scene, the large stage positioned in the rear of the club, and pushed her way to the front of the crowd. A man, a whip dangling from his hand, stood several feet away from the bound woman before him. The redheaded victim's hands were tied over her head to the whipping post, her legs spread out by an iron bar shackled to her ankles. She had no recourse. Nothing for her to do but to accept the lashes of the man holding the braided whip.

Azalea focused on him. He wore only a pair of black slacks. She would have expected leather. His chest was completely bared to the audience except for the large tattoos covering his arms and pecs. He could have been one of the sculpted statues decorating the club, with his chiseled features and body. Everything about him appeared hard. Unyielding.

And the tent in his pants proved it.

"He better finish her off soon." A whisper came from behind her. "I need to get you upstairs or I'm going to fucking come in my pants."

Azalea glanced over her shoulder at the man who spoke. His eyes met hers briefly, and he grinned, pressing a kiss to the temple of the woman beside him. She appeared as aroused as her partner with her dilated eyes and her teeth biting her bottom lip.

When Azalea looked back up at the scene, her eyes caught in the man with the whip's gaze. Her breath snagged, and she swallowed back a surprised gasp. He stared right at her, a deep crease building in his brow.

Such power, and it centered on her. Her breath came easier when he turned back to the woman on the post.

Six crimson welts crossed the woman's slender back. Her forehead rested on the wooden pole, her muscles tight and waiting for the next lash.

The man circled her, watching her with his dark gaze; his brow furrowed. Azalea bit down on her lip as he stood before the whipped woman and pinched her nipples. A seductive moan crossed the stage and over the audience.

"One more for my girl," he announced and released her breasts.

Azalea covered her mouth when he retook his position and pulled his hand back. She forced herself not to look away. His muscles rippled with his movement, his eyes stayed focused on his target, and the whip landed with precision. Another red mark bloomed on the creamy flesh, and the woman screamed, throwing her head from side to side.

He hung the whip around his neck and went to her, lightly tracing each mark with his fingers before placing a soft kiss to it. The crowd dispersed, moving back to whatever games they had been playing on their own or heading to the bar for more indulgence. Azalea stayed. She watched, mesmerized by the tender care he gave his tortured prey.

The man who'd whipped her with such power, such precision, brought her down from the pole and wrapped a blanket around her. Azalea caught the tiny wince she gave at having her back touched, but she also noted the sated look on her beautiful face. The man who had wielded the whip escorted her to the side of the stage and handed her off to another man who led the woman behind the curtains.

Something so intense, so barbaric in nature hadn't been cruel at all. Azalea sighed to herself. If she'd arrived earlier, she could have seen more, but it had been hard enough getting out without being noticed. If she had left any earlier, her mother would have been informed. The guards would have seen her leave and tattled right away.

Once the man with the tattoos disappeared, Azalea headed to the bar. One drink and a small amount of voyeurism, and she'd head back home. If her mother caught her, it would be months before she could revisit the club.

She ran her fingers through her long locks and pulled them forward over her shoulder, covering most of her chest with her golden hair.

"What can I get you?" the bartender, a youngish man with a black skull tattooed across his throat asked.

"A glass of wine? White please?" She wedged her way between two couples and found a stool. The scenes along the wall in the alcoves changed. The trussed-up woman was let out of her bonds, and another couple moved into the area to start a new scene.

"Fantastic, isn't it?" the bartender asked as he slid her wine to her. "You've never been in here before."

"No." She shook her head and handed money across the bar.

He shook his head. "No charge." He smiled and pointed toward the main stage. "But Peter wants a word."

"Peter?" she asked, looking where he had pointed. The man who had done the whipping stood center stage, glaring at her over the heads of the crowd. "Why?"

"Probably because you're not allowed in here." The bartender laughed, tapped the bar with his knuckles, and moved on. "Finish your drink. You'll need it."

Azalea tugged up on the neckline of the dress she wore, suddenly aware of the eyes preying on her. She'd only been able to grab something from her closet, and the deep purple dress had been the only one that seemed fitting for the club. And the only dress that fit, even poorly. Although the neckline was deep, all of her was covered. The skirt of the dress went far past her knees. Overall, she wasn't much to look at. Not in comparison to the beautiful women of the Tower.

She decided not to be afraid. She'd come this far; she wasn't going to let a little glare from across the room set her spine on fire.

Even if it did.

Sipping her wine, she turned away from the dark figure looming over the crowd. If he wanted to speak to her, he could damn well come down from his spotlight and do so. She wouldn't be afraid. She had every right to be there.

Unless he knew her mother.

If he knew her mother, her being there in his club could be more dangerous than she'd bargained for when she'd descended the back stairwell of her house.

Familiar anger brewed within her. When would she ever get a say? She was tired of being pulled and yanked in whatever direction her mother wanted. And now it seemed she had men all over the city waiting for her to make a mistake.

Well, enough was enough. She put her empty glass on the counter and spun around with the intent to march through the crowd and tell Peter whatever-his-name-was to go to hell.

Only, when she turned, she smacked right into him. Peter. The bare-chested, glowering man had come through the crowd and right up to her without her so much as sensing him.

"Dammit." She rubbed her nose that had been smashed in the collision.

"You shouldn't be in here." His deep voice vibrated through the noise. "If you want to work my club, you enter through the back entrance and you get assigned a handler."

Work his club?

"What are you talking about?" She tried to retreat, but the crowd kept her pinned against him. "I'm not—oh my god—

you think I'm one of the girls?" She covered her mouth to hide the nervous giggle starting to erupt. Her most annoying flaw, the stupid giggle. "I'm not. I just wanted to see the club. I'm not working—for anyone."

He narrowed his gaze as it traveled down the length of her body. She tugged on her neckline again, not that it would do much good.

"You're alone?" The accusation of being single came harsher than the accusation of being a working girl in his club.

"Yes." She nodded, raising her chin. She wouldn't cower. Not anymore.

Peter moved his gaze from her, over to the bartender. "Two drink max. Put it on the house tab," he said, holding up two fingers.

"Are you trying to dictate how much I have to drink?" She didn't bother trying to hide her annoyance at his arrogance.

"No." He settled his dark stare on her. "I'm not *trying* to do anything. I'm doing it. Two drinks, that's all. And if anyone approaches you that you don't want, you signal that guy over there." Peter turned to point at a security guard standing at the end of the bar.

"I can handle myself perfectly fine." She curled her toes in her shoes. If that were the actual truth, she wouldn't be in her current situation.

The right side of his lips curled up. Not a true smile, but at least his expression lightened.

"I'm sure that's true—uh, what's your name?" He leaned closer to hear her, but in doing so he brought his manly scent with him. She inhaled deeply, enjoying the musk and leather smell.

"Azalea," she said softly.

He pulled back with a wrinkled brow. "How unusual."

"It's a flower. My mother has a thing for flowers," she explained.

"Hmm." He pressed his lips together. "Well, Azalea, you've already had one drink. You can have one more for the night."

"You can't go bossing around girls you don't even know," she snarled. She had already planned on having maybe one more glass of wine, if that, but she couldn't allow his arrogance to go unchecked.

He quirked a black eyebrow at her, making his earlier glare seem like a pleasant greeting. "This is my club. If I say two drinks, then it's two drinks. I could say no more. Would that get the message through clearer?"

She squared her shoulders to meet him head-on. She'd never see him again after this. Why not push the boundary just a little? Why not have a tiny bit of fun before she found herself locked away again?

"And if I have more? I could easily get one of these men to buy me a drink." She waved a hand, gesturing to the crowd. Obviously, a single woman in the club was a rare thing, so it was an easy bet the men would fall at her feet if she asked.

His eyes narrowing a fraction, he placed his hands on the bar behind her, pinning her with a steely gaze.

"I don't think you want to know what the consequence for disobedience would be."

She gave a purposeful glance at the empty stage. "I think I may have an idea."

His lips curved into a broad smile, like her statement pleased him almost as much as her cheek annoyed him.

"What you saw was play. A little show for the club."

Azalea sensed the darkness in him, in the way his smile twisted and his brow quirked when he gave the veiled threat. A part of her should have been leery, scared even, but she found herself wanting to step into it with him. To be devoured, if only for a brief moment, by the darkness in him.

"Two drinks. Not a sip more. It's for your safety, Azalea, not because I'm an ass." He tapped the tip of her nose with his finger and stood back, giving her more air to breathe, more space to get lost in.

"And you put safety above profits for all your customers?" she pressed him.

"Only those worthy," he quipped and gestured to the bartender. "She's cut off after one more glass of wine. If you serve her, or any man that gives her a drink, you'll be fired, on the spot, with no reference."

Azalea gasped and looked at the bartender to gauge his response.

To her surprise, he only nodded. "Got it. One more glass of white then cut off."

"That's not fair. How could he know if someone is buying a drink for me?" she demanded of Peter.

He shifted his black gaze back to her and lifted a shoulder in an easy shrug. "Life is often that way, princess."

She couldn't logically argue the point. She knew that lesson well enough already.

"Maybe you are an ass, after all," she retorted, and he laughed, a soft chuckle really, but it lightened his features.

"I never said I wasn't. I only said that wasn't the reason I'm cutting you off."

The man was impossible, and he was wasting all of her time. She didn't have long before she needed to hightail it back home.

"Whatever." She rolled her eyes and turned her back on him, signaling to the bartender that she would like to have that last glass of wine. She didn't really want it. But she wasn't going to let the overgrown ape behind her think he actually had a say in what she did or didn't do.

"I think someone really wants a spanking tonight." His deep whisper ran along her ear. "You don't have to be so naughty. If you want to play, come up to my office. The guard will let you in, and I'll give you all the spankings you'd like. But if you keep being so bad, I won't be able to make you feel good."

She froze. Every muscle in her body refused to move. How the hell was she supposed to respond to that. Obviously, she couldn't.

Right?

No, she couldn't.

She didn't have time.

And especially not with him.

Too arrogant.

Too handsome.

Too dominating.

"Maybe, if I have time." She tried to sound dismissive, but she could feel the tremor in her voice. Hopefully, the sound was lost in the background noise.

"Well, I hope you do."

She picked up her fresh glass of wine and turned back to him. But he was gone. She spotted him in the crowd; the sea of people simply parted for him as he made his way through. He jogged up the steps near the stage and stopped to speak to the guard. She noticed him point in her direction, and her cheeks heated. He really wanted her to go to his office?

For a spanking?

The small clutch hanging from her wrist vibrated.

"Shit," she muttered, put her glass back down, untouched, and dug out the watch. Her alarm reminded her of the time, and the urgency with which she needed to get her ass moving.

Half an hour. Just enough time to collect her coat and get home before her mother's meeting ended.

Forgetting the glass of wine, she pushed her way through the crowd and made for the exit.

CHAPTER 2

The windows rattled from the thunder outside. A storm brewed, and Peter wished it was only the weather that signified the shitstorm coming toward him.

He knew opening his club could be seen as a breakaway from the Annex, at least by members of town who didn't quite grasp the full concept of loyalty. Having his own piece of the nightlife didn't distract him from his family. His loyalty would always remain with the Titon family. But it did give him a place where he reigned absolutely. No one to answer to, no one to run things by, everything on his terms and within his control. Exactly the way he liked it.

Peter walked to the windows overlooking the city below. He'd invited a woman up to his office. A woman he didn't know but had been drawn to from his first glance at her in the crowd.

She played coy pretty well, but he had seen the nervousness buzzing beneath her fake glare. The more she thrust her chin up, the more visible the fear. The little tremble in her voice cemented the observation for him. She was an innocent. Hell, she could be a damn virgin with the way her eyes widened at the sights before her. But when he'd taken the whip to Cassandra during their little show for the club, Azalea had soaked it all in.

He had planned to take Cassandra up on her offer of dinner after their demonstration, but changed his mind when he caught Azalea's eye. Her clothing hugged her too tightly, presenting more of her body than someone not offering a sample would have, but she'd said she wasn't working.

Peter sighed and shook his head. She probably wouldn't be coming up. And he should be getting back to the Annex. With Ash away on his honeymoon, he had double duty to be sure the girls were safe and staying within their boundaries. Even grown women who knew damn well the consequences for breaking the safety rules of the house would play harder when the boss was away.

Making his way down through the back stairwell, he called the garage attendant and told him to have his car ready for him. The two-way mirror wall he descended past gave him the opportunity to overlook the dancing and playing going on in the club. He scanned the crowd for the stark-blond hair of Azalea, but came up with nothing. Maybe he'd scared her off, and maybe it was better for her to be gone. An innocent like her would be devoured.

"It's starting to come down hard." Sam left the door open to Peter's black Challenger to let him slide into the driver's seat.

"I'll be fine," Peter assured him with a grin. He could handle any car in any weather. The rain would make traffic more annoying not more dangerous.

"See you tomorrow, then." Sam waved and headed back to his post at the gates.

Pulling out, Peter threw on the wipers and made his way through traffic to Main Street. The rain messed up the already-overcrowded streets, and quickly brought him to a standstill. As he leaned back in his seat, sighing again at the exhaustion he felt in his muscles, he turned to watch the people on the sidewalk. He'd built as far from The Titon clubs as he could. Unfortunately, that meant a less exclusive part of the city. Although street crime was well managed around his club, he saw to that, he didn't like the surrounding neighborhood.

A flash of white caught his eye, and he inched forward, ducking his head to get a better view. The dark hood flew off a woman running toward his car, and all of the blond hair hiding beneath tumbled out. She grabbed for the hood while trying to jog through the crowd, but wasn't finding much success.

"What the hell is she doing?" He was already several blocks away from Tower, far from the reach of any of the security guards or the extra police presence he demanded. The wind whipped her hair in front of her, and she swiped it away, still stuck behind a group of people not getting the idea she seemed to be in a hurry.

Peter found an alley entrance and blew his horn while merging through traffic to get to it. He pulled into the alleyway, cutting off the group from crossing. A few men in the crowd flicked him off and cursed, but once he stepped out of the car, they backed off, walked around the back of the Challenger, and moved on.

Azalea still struggled with her coat and the whipping wind and acknowledged seeing him. Peter approached her and grabbed her arms.

She shrieked and looked up at him, wild fear dancing in her eyes.

"It's me, Peter—from Tower," he said, pulling her closer to his car. "You don't have a ride?"

She blinked a few times, her hair so wet it stuck to her

forehead.

"No—I was going to take the bus, but—"

He shook his head. "I'll drive you. Get in."

She looked to the car then back to the road. "The bus—"

"Stopped running five minutes ago. Didn't you check the schedule?" One of the many things he hated about public transportation. With all the new taxi and car services, the busses stopped running before most of the clubs even slowed down in the evening.

A clap of thunder cut her response off, and he shook his head. "Tell me in the car. You're not walking, or rather running, in this." Her cloak opened up a bit, and her already-too-tight dress clung to her as a second skin, and water droplets glistened off her exposed cleavage. Fuck, his cock reacted too quickly to her.

She opened her mouth, probably to try and protest again, but snapped it shut as a bolt of lightning illuminated the night sky. With a nod, she pushed forward and let him lead her to the passenger side.

Once back in the car, he resituated himself. Soaked through, he looked over at her. "Buckle up," he reminded her when she hadn't moved to grab the belt.

"Is that time correct?" she asked pointing at the digital clock on the dash, which showed 11:45 p.m.

"Yeah, why?"

She snagged the belt and secured it. "I live four miles down Main Street. Corner of Main and 3rd." She pointed at the alleyway. "I think if you go through here and take back roads, it will be faster than turning around on Main." She looked behind her, out the rear window. "Traffic looks bad."

He listened to her rambling and suspected it wasn't from fear of him, but panic about time. Her response to his invitation had been, *If I have time*.

"Do you have a curfew or something?" he asked, throwing the car into drive and getting them moving.

"What? No. I just—I really need to get home."

Even with her innocent aura, she didn't appear underage. And his doorman wouldn't have let her inside Tower if she wasn't at least drinking age. Since he'd already jumped to the conclusion she was a working girl in his club uninvited, he wasn't looking to offend her again by demanding to see her ID.

Peter knew the city well enough to stay off the overcrowded streets.

"You weren't at Tower very long," he said, increasing the speed of the wipers. The rain pelted the car as he made his way toward her house.

"I underestimated how long it would take to get there." She glanced his way then turned to stare out her window. "I saw enough, I think."

"Cassandra. She's the woman I was working with on stage. She's all right. She's not hurt." He never explained his sort of play with anyone, but then again, he couldn't recall the last time he'd encountered someone who didn't understand.

"I know." Azalea pulled her hair from behind her and ran her fingers through the long tresses. "She looked—happy."

Peter smiled. Cassandra would have been happier if he'd given her half a dozen more lashes with the whip, but he knew when enough was enough. Endorphins sometimes fuzzed the truth of what a submissive could take.

"I knew what I would see at the club. So, if you're worried you scared me or something, don't be." She leaned forward in her seat. "I'm getting your car all wet."

Peter made a right turn and flipped the vents to blow more on her side of the car. "What were you doing, trying to run home?"

"It's really none of your concern," she said, splaying her hands in front of the hot air blowing at her.

"Do you know what kind of people hang out on that corner you were coming up on?"

"If the area is so bad, why put your club there?" she countered.

He let the question pass. He could go into a long speech about wanting to revive the area. Bring it up to a better standard for those living and working in it. The women slinging sex on the street needed safer places to work.

Not that he considered himself the savior of women, or anyone for that matter. Hell, he wouldn't be accused by anyone of having a heart of gold. But people deserved better.

"So, no cab money?" He pushed the subject again.

She didn't answer, only huffed and scratched her neck. He let her stew in her soaked clothing while he made his way through town. She glanced at the digital clock over and over again, her fingers twisting together every time another minute clicked off.

"Go through the alley. It's faster." She pointed at the narrow opening coming up on his right side.

He flipped on his signal and made the turn.

"Now a left. I'm right on the corner," she said, already gathering her belongings and grasping on the handle.

"Hold on, Azalea. Don't jump out." He found an open spot to pull into and hopped out, thankful the rained had died down to an annoying mist, and ran to her side.

"I could have done that." She stepped from the car and pulled her cloak tighter around her body.

"I think the words you meant to say were thank you," he chided in a low tone, taking a step toward her. It was one thing for her to get riled after he accused her of being a hooker, but being rude for the sake of being rude didn't fly with him.

He blocked her from moving away from the car and towered over her. She let out a hard sigh and dropped her shoulders.

"Thank you. For the wine. For the insults. And for the ride." She looked up at him, the innocent eyes he'd been drawn to at the club narrowed, and her lips pressed together. "I really need to go." A tremor underlay her voice. She wasn't irritated with him, she was getting panicked.

"Next time I see you, we can have a long chat about manners and the proper way of thanking me." He pushed his lips up into a grin and strode out of her way, following her as she approached the stairs of the brownstone.

She stopped on the first step and turned to face him. "You don't have to walk me up. I'm good from here."

The lace drapes covering the front window moved to the side then dropped back into place.

Peter sensed her urgency, felt the tension building inside her, and stepped back onto the sidewalk. He'd stay back, but he wasn't walking away. The air didn't smell right, didn't feel right. Something here was wrong.

"I'll wait until you're inside," he said flatly. She wouldn't be able to convince him otherwise, and hopefully she understood that from his tone.

The click of a lock being undone grabbed her attention, and she spared a second to glare at him then turned and shuffled up the stairs. As soon as the door started to open, she rushed through.

She made it inside before Peter could see who opened it, but not before he heard the threatening voice greeting her.

"You barely made it home. How the hell did you get out this time?" The door shut on Azalea's response, but Peter doubted her words would have shed any light on the situation anyway.

What the hell did he mean how did she get out?

The rain came faster and harder, again, but he stood where he was, watching the windows. A light flickered to life on the top floor. A small, single bulb burned behind the shade. It was her. He could make out her figure; she brushed her hair out as she paced in front of the window.

He shook his head, reminding himself, whatever her problem was, it was hers. He didn't know her and didn't owe her anything.

He did the right thing, brought her home. Didn't let her run in the rain through a shitty part of town.

So why, as he pulled his car away from the brownstone, was he more worried about her now than when he found her on the street?

CHAPTER 3

"Azalea, you look exhausted," her mother admonished at the breakfast table.

"I didn't sleep well," Azalea said, not lying in the least. Her heart had been jackhammering after leaving Peter outside of her house and hightailing inside. Her mother had walked in the back door only moments later. If Peter had kept insisting on walking her up to the door, they would have been found.

She could feel her mother staring at her, judging and evaluating her, from her seat across the table. Her long fingers fondled the handle of her coffee cup.

"You were up late?" she asked. To anyone listening it might sound merely curious. Azalea was, after all, an adult, and didn't have a bedtime, but she knew the tones well. She was fishing. She suspected, and Azalea knew what would happen if her mother found out she'd managed to slip out of the house after she'd left for her meeting.

"I was reading," Azalea lied and took a bite of her toast.

Her mother sighed but left it alone. "You love those books more than me, I think."

Azalea smiled. "Of course not." As much as some of her

moods held Azalea at arm's length, she knew her mother needed to feel her love. Insecurity would run deep in anyone who had lost a child and had a man simply walk out of her life like it was the easiest thing to do. Azalea never met or knew much about her father, other than that he'd found out her mother was pregnant for a second time and disappeared.

"Good." She reached across the table and patted Azalea's hand. "I have to leave town for the yearly meeting earlier than usual. I'm leaving tomorrow morning."

Her mother never fully explained what she did at these meetings, or exactly how she earned her money. But given the fact that Azalea never wanted for anything material, she didn't push the issue.

"How long will you be gone?" Azalea asked, already concocting day trips to the museums. It wouldn't be difficult with her mother gone during the day; she'd have to have Santos accompany her. But there were also the evenings. When she was supposed to be tucked into the house—for her own safety—she wanted to explore the city. That would be harder, but not impossible. And having her mother gone would make it even easier.

"Three weeks, maybe a little more," her mother said. Her fingers started drumming on the tabletop. "I'll be home in time for your birthday."

Azalea watched her expression carefully. Every time she mentioned her birthday, her lips tightened. It was as though she was trying to keep back excitement, or maybe it was fear. She always warned Azalea of the dangers in the city, and promised that when the time came for her to finally move out of the house and start her own life, she would be with her every step of the way. Nearing her twenty-third birthday, it seemed that should be right around the corner.

"I was thinking." Azalea placed her fork down and folded her hands in her lap. "When you return from your meeting, we could start looking for an apartment for me. I've already graduated. I have my degree. Maybe it's time I look for a job, start making my own money. Like we talked about?"

"You have everything you need or could want right here. Why would you want to go work for someone else? Slave away to make them richer while you get by on a meager paycheck?"

"Maybe you could teach me about what you do."

Santos, always watching, stifled a cough behind her. Obviously, he found the idea funny. Well he could go sit and spin, for all Azalea cared. She wasn't stupid. Maybe a little over-sheltered, but she had a good head on her shoulders. And her damn near-perfect GPA backed her up.

Bellatrix's eyes fluttered from Santos to Azalea before a well-practiced smile perched on her lips. "Azalea, I'm not sure your degree in graphic design can—uh—well, be put to use in my business. But, I suppose I can understand you wanting to spread your wings a bit. You'll be twenty-three next month, and I remember wanting the same when I was your age. When I get home, we'll discuss it further. But until then, no more worrying about the future. All right?"

"Of course," Azalea answered in the soft tone she'd become used to using with her mother. Bellatrix demanded respect from her employees and wanted undying love from her daughter.

"Good. What do you have planned for today? I will be busy most of the day, but we could meet for dinner?"

"Oh, can we go out? I heard there's a new restaurant opening up on the waterfront." Azalea clamped down on her excitement at the prospect of getting out into the nightlife, hoping her mother wouldn't see how much she truly wanted to go.

"And where did you hear this?" Bellatrix asked and sipped her coffee.

"When I was at the library yesterday afternoon. The librarian was talking about it with the woman checking out books. She said it was the best meal she'd had in years." Azalea paraphrased the librarian's actual review of the meal as orgasmic.

"Perhaps we'll go when I get back from my trip." Bellatrix stood from the table and ran her long fingers over her waist then down her pantlegs, smoothing out all unwanted wrinkles. "Enjoy your day, dear." She pressed a warm kiss to Azalea's temple and headed out of the dining room.

Azalea sank back into her chair and let out a long whoosh of breath. No matter how much her mother doted on her, how much she professed to love her, Azalea often had a lingering darkness hovering over her whenever her mother was near.

"While your mother is away, you will not cause me trouble," Santos said from his place at the door. Still standing guard, but most likely more to keep her in than to keep others out.

"I never do." She rolled her eyes and picked up her cup of coffee.

He laughed. "I have important business, and your little field trips are getting annoying."

Azalea dropped her napkin on her plate and walked to the door, pausing before him. "You heard her. When she gets back, we'll be looking for an apartment for me. Then you won't have to be bothered with me at all."

Santos's chest rumbled with a new laugh, darker this time. Meaner. "She'll never let you go. You're a fool."

"My mother wants what's best for me." Azalea straightened her back. "That's all. She's just a little insecure."

Santos's smile faded on the edges. "Bellatrix Gothel is many things, but insecure is not one of them. You'd do yourself a favor if you'd start seeing things that are right in front of you."

The power of the warning in his tone pushed her back a step, her eyes widened. Santos was a man to be feared, she knew that, could see it in his set jaw and the way her mother put so much of her trust in him to keep them both safe. But she'd never felt his power so easily before.

"I'm going to the park today."

"I'll have the car ready. Jackson will accompany you today. I have a meeting." He opened the door for her exit and, once she stepped out into the hall, he slammed it shut behind her.

A meeting.

Everyone around here had meetings except her.

There had to be more to life than such seclusion and so much dependency. Something electric and alive. Something that gave breath to her lungs.

Like how she'd felt riding in Peter's car.

Or how it felt when his body brushed up against hers, or when he talked.

Oh hell. She stalked up the stairs to her room to get her coat. She didn't have time for fairy-tale thoughts.

She had plans to make.

CHAPTER 4

"Hey, boss." Daniel walked into Ash's office where Peter sat at the desk going over business ledgers.

Ash had picked a great fucking time to go on his damn honeymoon. With Peter's club picking up business and the Annex gaining in popularity in conjunction, there was more paperwork to give Peter a fucking headache.

"I hate when you call me that." Peter tossed the pen onto the desk and rubbed his eyes. Ash needed to move away from paper ledgers and onto a damn computer system. Computers that had automatic calculations built in and wouldn't force Peter to have to remember math skills he'd long forgotten.

Daniel paused. "Well, unless you're promoting me to partner, that's what you are."

Peter blinked a few times and let out an exaggerated sigh. "Did you want something or just felt like coming in here to piss me off?"

Daniel laughed in response and finished his trek to the wet bar in the corner of the room. "I'm heading out in a few minutes with Johnny and Travis. A collection visit. I wanted to be sure we had the address right before we took off."

Peter's ears perked up. It had been months since he'd gone on a collection call. Since he put his mark on the city with Tower, he'd only been putting half the time into the Titon businesses. Including his collection responsibilities.

His cousin Ash had given his blessing for both the club and his reduction in duties at the house and Annex, but it didn't lessen the sense of guilt building within Peter. They were family. He couldn't completely abandon Ash to depend on the other men; they weren't blood.

"What's the debt?" Peter asked, slamming the Annex ledger closed and opening the drawer to dig out the one he wanted. Personal loans still brought in top dollar, and Peter didn't see Ash closing up shop anytime soon. But the money didn't come in if the clients didn't pay back the loans with a low interest rate to cover the risk.

"Hundred thousand. Richard Santos. He's two weeks behind." Daniel downed two fingers of whiskey and poured another.

Peter flipped to the page with Santos's debt and ran his finger along the line to his address. Ash needed more secure bookkeeping. A casual looker would see what appeared to be an address book. Names, addresses, phone numbers were all laid out openly. At first glance. But if a cop got his hands on it, they'd figure out pretty easily the phone numbers weren't real. They'd realize they translated to the original amounts of the loans and the percentages of the interest.

"Here it is. Six hundred North Main Street," Peter read out loud. He looked up at Daniel then back to the book. "Is that right?"

"If that's what it says." Daniel shrugged.

When Peter decoded the address to mean the real address was 300 South Main, he sat back in his chair and scratched his chin.

"Richard Santos? What's he do?"

Daniel shrugged again. "Hell if I know. He met Ash at Sampson's, asked for the cash, and Ash gave it."

"You need to pay more attention to the damn details, Daniel," Peter chastised. "You can't be the hired gun anymore."

Daniel's eyes went wide. "You usually handled that stuff. I'm just filling in here."

"You aren't filling in." Peter stood from the desk. "You're taking my place with this shit. I can't be handling collections, keeping watch on the girls in the Annex, and running my fucking club. You wanted more responsibilities, remember? And now you have them." Peter buttoned his jacket and made his way to the bar. A whiskey sounded fucking good.

"I wanted to work the Annex," Daniel said with some force.

"Well, you can't keep your dick out of the girls, so you can't be running shit over here," Peter shot back with more authority.

"Like you never fucked any of the girls."

"I haven't." Peter faced off with his longtime friend. "I keep my dick away from the Annex because those girls depend on me to keep them safe. I'm their fucking boss, Daniel. And I don't fuck my employees."

"I've never once taken advantage of the girls." Daniel squared off, rolling his shoulders back in defense.

"I didn't say you did. I'm saying you can't take responsibility for them if you keep fucking them." Peter poured himself a drink and threw it back, letting the heat slide down his throat to his belly. "So, in the meantime, you have this shit to deal with."

Daniel put his glass down on the bar. His jaw clenched, but he didn't continue the conversation. Daniel would lay his life on the line for the family. He was as close to family as an outsider could be, but he thought more with his cock than his head when it came to the girls. And until he could get that under control, he wouldn't be in charge of the Annex.

"I could use the distraction, I'll tag along with you." Peter left his glass on the bar and went back to the book to double-check the address. He didn't mention he knew the building. He'd just gotten done giving Daniel a hard time about mixing his carnal desires with business, and here he was doing the same damn thing.

"I don't need the help," Daniel said. Peter had ruffled his feathers.

"I know. I need a break from all these fucking numbers." Peter shut the book and opened the drawer to the right, grabbing the pistol stored there and adding it to his waistline.

Daniel looked him over slow, like he was sizing him up. Peter didn't let it get under his skin. He'd known Daniel long enough to know he was making sure his boss wasn't blowing smoke up his ass. Not that he'd done it in the past, but no matter how long Daniel was with the family, he was always suspicious of anyone offering anything in the name of help.

"Yeah, okay. Let's go."

Peter nodded and followed him out. Daniel could take the lead on this. Peter's intentions had nothing to do with the cash. He had a bigger prize in mind.

PETER FOLLOWED the three men up the steps to the front door. He looked up at the familiar window, checking for signs of her. The light was on, but no shadows were being cast like a few nights before.

Daniel explained to the asshole who opened the door they wouldn't be leaving until they spoke with Santos, and the little weasel of a man paled and let them in. Not much protection there.

"Daniel." A man, looking ten years older than the collector walked into the front hall, arms open in greeting and wide smile plastered on his dark lips. His beady eyes narrowed slightly, betraying his proposed hospitality.

"You remember me." Daniel ignored the outstretched arms and stood firm. "So, there's nothing wrong with your memory. Good. You remember the last conversation we had? About a week ago, when we met at Sampson's?"

Peter let the other man do his thing, while he looked up the stairs, half expecting to see a blond head pop out around the corner to listen. He stepped around his men and approached a closed door on the right.

"I said I'll get the money, and I will. I almost have all of it, just need another day or two," Santos said behind Peter.

Peter turned the knob on the door and realized it was locked. From the outside. He looked over his shoulder at the scene playing out. Daniel had it under control, so he walked a little farther down the hall.

"What's he doing?" Santo's asked.

"Never mind what he's doing," Daniel barked. "You focus on finding the money you owe. Time's up."

Another door stood at the end of the hall. It also was locked from the other side. Where the fuck was Azalea?

"'Let's get out of the hallway." Peter gestured to the first locked door he'd found. "Open this door, Santos." He tugged on the knob.

Santos swallowed hard. "Give me a minute and I'll get the fucking money," he said with a bitterness to his tone. Like a spoiled child who'd been told he couldn't have a third helping of his birthday cake.

"Great. We'll wait for you in there while Travis here escorts you to where you have it." Daniel moved his jacket back to expose his gun. He wouldn't pull it out unless more force was needed.

Santos eyed the room like he was making a decision.

"I wasn't asking," Daniel said in a deeper voice, one that left no room for negotiation or question. If Santos didn't get moving, there would be hell to pay.

After letting a soft curse out under his breath, Santos reached into his pocket and produced a key. Peter moved to the side to let him open the door, but once it was open, he pushed past him to get inside.

A sitting room. A bit fancy for Peter's taste with all the tapestry and French decor, but still just a room. So why the hell had it been locked?

"Thanks. We'll wait here," Daniel said. "Travis, help Mr. Santos locate his money. And don't hesitate to help him along if needed."

Travis sneered. "You got it."

Once Santos left the room with Travis, Daniel turned to Johnny. "Wait out in the hall and watch for them. I don't trust that asshole and we don't need any surprises."

"Got it." Johnny went back out into the hall.

Peter inspected the paintings on the walls. Portraits. Each of the same woman in several different poses. The woman bore little resemblance to Azalea. In contrast to Azalea's nearly white-blond hair, this woman's was thick and dark. Even her eyes were dark, unlike the large blue of Azalea's.

"This Santos asshole lives here or owns this place?" Peter asked when he finally came across a small photo of Azalea. A much younger girl when the photo was taken, but she had a bright smile on her lips, her eyes wide with joy, while the woman sitting next to her remained as stoic and serene as the paintings.

"He lives here, but works for some woman. Don't know much about her, though."

Peter looked harder at the portrait. A strong familiarity

came with her eyes. The little wrinkle around them, he'd seen it before, but he couldn't place the memory.

Since Ash had dropped out of the businesses his own father had been in, Peter hadn't kept track of the goings on of the other families in town. Maybe he'd seen her at a meeting or a party somewhere along the line. If that was true, that meant she worked with one of the other controlling families, and what he was going to do could cause more trouble than Ash would forgive him for.

But that fucking door was locked.

When Santos returned with Travis, Santos had several stacks of cash in his hands. "I'm short ten grand." He shoved the money at Daniel.

"Short?" Daniel arched a brow.

"I checked his room myself. He doesn't have it."

"Well—"

"Where's the girl?" Peter stepped forward.

"What girl?" If he hadn't tensed his jaw before asking the question, he might have been able to get away with his innocent reaction. But Peter had been watching men lie his entire life.

"The one you have locked up somewhere in this fucking house, asshole. Where is she?"

"She's not your concern," Santos said, with heat. Ah, maybe there was more to his job duties than being a dancing monkey for his boss.

"She is now. Go get her." Peter folded his arms over his chest. He'd wait, patiently, for about another thirty seconds.

"Jackson," Santos called out, keeping his stare fixed on Peter.

Another man, smaller in stature but not in attitude, appeared in the doorway. Where the hell had he come from?

"Go get Azalea."

"Santos." The warning in Jackson's voice solidified Peter's decision.

"Now." Peter gave the direction himself. "Get her and bring her down here." He pulled out his gun, holding it loosely at his side. "I'm out of patience with you assholes."

The room stayed silent as Jackson disappeared. If Daniel disapproved of Peter stepping in, he kept it to himself.

A door down the hall clicked opened and closed. It had to be the locked one he'd found. His jaw clenched, but he kept his glare focused on Santos, whose color slowly drained from his face.

The door shut again and Azalea appeared in the doorway.

"What's going on?" she asked. She surveyed the room, taking in the scene before her. "Peter?" She stopped at him.

"Ten grand, is that right, Santos?" Peter ignored her presence and focused on the scum standing before him.

"Ten." He nodded, his little eyes scanning over to Azalea then back at him. "She's not mine."

"I know." Peter holstered his gun. "She's mine, now."

"I mean, she's not mine to give," Santos said, this time turning his head toward her. "Tell him, Azalea."

"I didn't ask her opinion. I don't give a fuck who she belonged to before, she's mine, now, and the ten grand is forgiven."

"What are you talking about?" Azalea stepped farther into the room. "I'm not going with you."

Peter still didn't look at her.

"I can't let you take her." Santos trod forward, more of a plea for understanding than a threat, but Daniel yanked his gun out and trained it on him.

"You don't *let* us do anything, you asshole. She's coming with us. Whatever your issues with that-—are yours, and I don't give a flying fuck."

Peter walked behind Daniel and gave Travis and Johnny a

nod. They'd stand down unless Daniel needed help, which he wouldn't.

"I'm not going with you," Azalea said in a demanding voice. He cupped her elbow, but she yanked free and jumped back. "I'm not going."

Peter strode closer to her, and when she retreated, he stepped again, walking her back against the wall. Leaning in closer, he inhaled her scent. The freshly washed, sweet scent of the innocent woman he was going to corrupt.

"Rule one, you don't tell me what you will and won't do." He grabbed her chin, pressing his fingers into her face until she winced. "You are coming with me. And you won't give me any fucking trouble, or what you saw at Tower the other night will be the tip of the iceberg for you when we get home."

Her eyes widened at his promise.

"You don't fucking understand," Santos said, panic lacing his words. "You can't fucking take her."

"Too late." Moving his hand from her face to her arm, Peter gripped her bicep and walked to the front door, dragging her along.

"No." She pulled back, but he didn't stop. He intensified his grip and yanked her along the way. "No! Peter! No!" she yelled and smacked at his hand.

Fear embedded her demands to be let go. Poor girl didn't realize how much more that made him want her.

When he got to his car, he pulled his gun back out and pressed it against her back until she stopped fighting him. "Get in the car, Azalea. If you get back out, if you run, you will regret it. I will keep you safe, but you have to fucking listen to me. Any deviation from my directions, and you'll find out the consequences."

"Safe?" she hissed. "You're kidnapping me!" she yelled into the chilled wind of the night.

Peter glanced around. No crowd had formed, but if she kept up her fit, the neighbors would come to investigate.

"Don't make me gag you. Get in the fucking car."

"No." She shook her head and tugged again. "Fuck you." She spat at him, missing his face but getting his shoulder.

"Not on your first night. But if you're really good, maybe tomorrow." He pulled away from her, pushing the barrel of his gun into her back. She stilled, but it wasn't enough. She'd spat at him!

He yanked on her dress, a flimsy cotton thing, until her ass was exposed. Round, pert...fucking perfect.

"Peter." She didn't yell this time, probably not wanting to draw attention to them now that her ass was on display to the neighborhood.

He brought his left hand back and landed it on her ass three times in a row, same spot, same severity, eliciting the same muffled screech from her with each one. The darkness of the night, and the cotton panties she wore hid the blush of her ass from him, but he knew it was there. Knew the heat had been created. She stopped struggling.

"Get in, Azalea, or do you need more motivation?"

"No."

He hadn't hurt her, not really. She was probably shocked that he'd done it. Hell, he was a little surprised, too. Middle of the street, in the middle of getting her out of that house while his men were still dealing with Santos, but it needed to be done.

She'd be feeling a hell of a lot more if she didn't cooperate soon.

He yanked the door open. "You keep that dress up at your hips. I want your spanked ass on the seat," he ordered when she smoothed the dress back down.

She glanced at him, anger shooting at him while she did as he told her.

"Asshole," she shot at him as he closed the door.

"You have no idea," he said, more to himself.

"Peter." Daniel jogged down the steps of the brownstone, Travis and Johnny following him. "You sure about that?" he asked, glancing at Azalea sitting in the car, her arms folded, her eyes focused straight ahead.

"What do you mean?"

"I mean—we don't usually steal women for debt," Daniel said quietly. Travis and Johnny made their way to Daniel's car without commenting.

"Don't worry about what I'm doing. You worry about getting that cash logged in, and I want a man stationed on this fucking house. I want to know the second Santos's boss gets back."

"Sure. Uh, what are you going to do with her?" He jerked a thumb at the car.

Peter didn't respond. He walked around the hood, keeping her in his side view as he made his way to his door and jerked it open.

She remained silent when he turned the ignition.

Daniel's question had merit.

What the hell was he going to do with her?

CHAPTER 5

The man obviously had a few screws loose in that head of his.

"You can't just take me," Azalea said after too many moments of silence stretched between them.

He grunted in response. A damn grunt. Maybe he was more animal than human.

"I mean it, Peter." Remembering the skirt of her dress was still hiked up over her hips, she grabbed the hem and wiggled it back down. She'd been too surprised at the short spanking to fight him at the moment, but his gun was no longer pointed at her, and her ass was safely pressed against the warm leather seat.

"Don't." His paw of a hand moved from the steering wheel to her own, gripping one hard and yanking it from its mission. "I want your ass on the seat. I want you to let it sink in that from this moment on, you'll do what I say or feel the consequences."

She stared at him, slack-jawed, while he kept his focus on the road stretching out in front of them. Yep. Bona fide crazy.

"Let me go," she demanded in the hardest voice she could conjure up. He ran his thumb over her knuckles before releasing her.

"Leave that dress the way you have it." He went back to gripping the wheel with both hands.

"You're a lunatic," she accused.

He gave a dark chuckle. "I've been called worse."

"Santos won't let you take me. He'll come for me." If only to save his own sorry skin, but he wouldn't let her disappear. Her mother would have his head.

"I doubt that, Azalea. He's a hired thug. You're his boss's daughter, isn't that right? He's probably already packed a bag and hightailed it out of town." Peter glanced over at her. "If he's smart, that's what he did."

The car jarred as it ran over a pothole, and she gripped the door handle. Her head spun.

Before Jackson had come into her room demanding she follow him downstairs, she'd been making plans to get out of the house the next evening. Now, it seemed she was out, and she needed to figure a way to get back in.

"What do you want with me?" she asked, folding her hands over her lap. Her thighs were completely bare, with her dress hiked up around her waist. The spanking hadn't hurt, not really. A few swats to her ass had been enough to shock her, but there wasn't much pain. The tingle it sent through her body bothered her more than the brief sting of his hand.

She shouldn't have a tingle. She shouldn't have anything except anger and contempt for the asshole stealing her.

"Not your concern at the moment," he answered and turned off the main road and onto an access drive.

As he drove up the winding road, a mansion came into view. With the dark night blanketing the background, the lighted windows sent a shiver through her. She recognized the mansion, its peaks visible from her bedroom window, and there were pictures of it in the papers from time to time. Ash Titan lived there.

She'd heard murmurs among her mother's men about what went on inside the walls of the Annex. Women were auctioned off, contracted out for deviant play and sex. Women sold from one man to another for whatever pleasure their new owners desired.

And Peter was taking her there.

He'd said the debt had been forgiven. That's what he'd told Santos when he took her. He was going to sell her to repay a debt? Whose debt?

She closed her eyes for a moment and swallowed back rising panic. Nothing ever got accomplished by crying. She wouldn't allow this. She was so close to gaining some freedom. Her mother was finally going to let her move out. She was finally going to have a life of her own.

As soon as he parked, she moved into action. She flipped the lock and threw open the door, jumping out of the car before Peter could grab her.

"Hey!"

She heard him yell for her, but she didn't stop. She raced down the cobblestone path to the gates they'd driven through. If she ran fast enough, she could get through before they closed. But they were already moving, the moonlight flickering off the metal as they crept closer to one another.

"Azalea!" He sounded closer.

She pumped her arms and pushed herself to move, to get there, to get out, to get away from the Annex and from Peter.

"Goddammit! Grab her!"

A man appeared from out of the little house near the gate. She hadn't seen him before. Had he been there?

She shrieked and tried to jolt around him, but he was in front of her and his hands were on her, holding her arms tight. She fought against him, kicked at him, but the damn mammoth didn't even flinch.

With another cry of frustration, she watched the gates come together. The bolt latching echoed in the courtyard. She was stuck.

"Where the hell did you think you were going?" Peter jogged up to her and gave the mammoth a nod, which she assumed meant he could release her, since he did. He didn't leave, though, instead, he blocked her from behind.

"I won't let you sell me." She took a step back, feeling the danger of the guard too close behind her. With nowhere to go, she could only gain a few inches of space between her and Peter, but it was enough to let her breathe easier.

Peter's lips thinned as he pressed them together. Each puff of air flared his nostrils, but he didn't say a word.

He snagged her hand and pulled her back up the driveway. She took deep breaths to calm her lungs, burning from the run, and to keep her heart from jumping out of her chest.

Fighting him wouldn't get her anywhere. Not with the mammoth at the gate, and who knew what other animals lurked inside the mansion to help him.

She managed to keep up with him as he took the steps up to the entrance, but when he pulled her to the large staircase inside, she resisted again.

"I'm not going up there," she said, shaking her head.

He sighed and spun to face her. "You are. Either you walk up these steps, or I throw you over my shoulder and carry you up. Either way is fine with me, but I'm sure you have a preference."

Azalea clenched her teeth. A smartass remark would probably give him a reason to make the decision for her, and she had a good idea which way he would choose.

She met his gaze, forcing herself to ignore the irritation lurking in his dark glare. "I'll walk on my own."

He released her hand and moved aside, waving her ahead of him.

Smoothing her dress, she raised her chin and climbed the staircase.

"If you run again, Azalea, I'll take my belt to your ass before you go to sleep. Go up one more floor," he said as they reached the landing.

She didn't respond to his threat. Although, she knew it was more of a promise—a hope even. She'd seen him whipping the woman at Tower. She'd seen his thrill as the whip landed and the woman cried out. If she ran again, it would give him a reason to take the leather strap to her. An idea that once made her reach into her panties and ease the ache, but facing his dark glare and set jaw, she didn't think the reality would match the fantasy.

When she reached the next floor, he moved past her and walked down the hall. She glanced back down the steps, but decided to follow him instead. He stopped outside a door and pulled a key from his pocket.

"The entire floor is mine." He slipped the key inside. "You'll stay in my bedroom for now." The lock clicked as it unlatched, and he pushed the door open.

He gestured for her to enter, but she couldn't quite make her feet move. Inside was a prison. Santos had barely argued about him taking her. He'd seemed fearful of Peter and his men, and she'd never seen Santos fear anything.

If she went in, he could lock her away. He could sell her to a monster who would beat her, rape her, and worse. Tears burned her eyes, but she took a deep breath and blinked them back. She wouldn't let him see her fear.

"Azalea, there's no decision to make here. Go in." His voice was velvety, his touch, when he placed his hand on her back, warm and almost soothing.

She nodded, straightened her back, and stepped inside.

Whatever was coming next, she would deal with it. She'd always learned how to cope, how to manage, and she would do it again.

She would not be sold.
She would not be owned.
She would be free.

ღ ღ ღ

PETER LEFT her to stew all alone in his bedroom. At first, relief had rushed through her when he hadn't entered with her before closing the door. But the reprieve quickly turned into a chokehold of uncertainty.

What if he came back with more men? What if he already had someone who wanted to buy her? She hadn't formed a plan yet. She hadn't had time.

She stared at the door, the intricately carved wooden door that under any other circumstance would appeal to her artistic side, both fearing and hoping it would open.

"Get a damn grip," she chastised herself, and sat on the hope chest at the foot of the king-sized four-poster bed. She noticed the woodwork on the bed matched that of the door. But she couldn't focus on things like design patterns. She needed to get her heart to stop trying to escape her chest.

The room held a more menacing feel than the outside of the mansion. All dark wood furniture with sharp angles and edges. All very masculine. Tall candlesticks lined the nearby dresser, and three candle sconces hung on the wall over the bed.

The furniture in the corner opposite the bed caught her attention. A black leather spanking bench in one corner, and a dark cherrywood cross in the opposite corner. Cuffs dangled from the cross.

She left the bed and inspected the cross. She'd seen it before in pictures and understood how it was used, but she'd never been so close to one. Running her hand over the thick beam, she closed her eyes, letting the smooth surface run along her palm.

"That's called a St. Andrew's Cross," Peter's deep voice announced. She hadn't heard him come in. Losing herself in a damn fantasy again, she hadn't noticed the door opening.

She dropped her hand from the beam and spun around. "I know what it is."

He arched his right brow. "I was hoping a few minutes alone would help you calm down." He stepped closer. "I suppose not."

"Calm down?" She fisted her hands at her sides. "You kidnapped me and are going to sell me to some monster who will do who knows what to me, and I'm supposed to calm down because you left me alone in a room with your torture equipment?" Years of maintaining her voice at an even level for her mother kept her from yelling at him, but if he lifted that eyebrow another centimeter, she wasn't sure she could stop herself.

"Torture?" He looked at the cross then made a pointed gesture of looking at the spanking bench. "I suppose, but it's the most delicious kind of torture, I assure you."

She stared at him. Was he making a joke? Did he think lightening the mood was going to help make her pliable?

"Where did you get the idea that you're being sold?" He unbuttoned his jacket with one hand.

"You brought me here. This is the Annex, right? Women are sold here." Did he think she was that ignorant to not know where he'd brought her?

"You have things twisted a bit there. You aren't here to be sold. I meant what I said to Santos. You're mine now."

"Yours?" She huffed a laugh. "Like I'm some toy on a shelf in the store?"

He shrugged out of his jacket and tossed it on the bed, making his way toward her.

"Why did Santos have your room locked?"

It took a moment for her to register the change in topic. She hadn't realized the door had been locked, but she wasn't surprised. With her mother gone, Santos had the burden of making sure she didn't wander around town, especially at night.

"It's a safety thing," she said, unsure why she felt the need to defend her mother's way of keeping her safe.

"A safety thing?" He unbuttoned the cuffs of his shirt and rolled each of them up to his elbows, exposing dark ink swirling across his forearms in patterns and words she couldn't make out from her position.

"The other night, you needed to get home in a hurry. Like you were some teenager breaking curfew. And tonight, I found you locked away in your room. What's going on over there on Main Street?" His jaw tensed and his stare molten when he finally met her gaze.

"N-nothing. My mother is overprotective." He would never understand.

"You're a little old to be living with an overprotective mother. And that doesn't explain why locking you away is for your safety. All I had to do was order Santos to get you, and you were served up. So, I'd say it had more to do with keeping you in, and less about keeping others out."

"Is that why you kidnapped me and locked me up here? To save me from some twisted version of my life you've built up in your head?"

He was only a pace away.

"I didn't lock the door, Azalea." He folded his arms over his chest. Without his jacket to hide his physique, she could make out the built muscles of his shoulders and his chest. She wondered if the tattoos ran all the way up his arms and how much more of him they covered.

"What?"

"I didn't lock the door. But it's interesting that you assumed you'd be locked in."

Of course, she assumed it. He was keeping her captive. Why the hell wouldn't he have locked the damn door?

She closed her eyes and took a slow breath. "Just-I—Take me home, Peter. My mother will pay the money Santos owes you. You don't have to do this."

"Your mother. Another topic for discussion. But not yet. Not tonight. Tonight, you need rest." He didn't move, but she could feel him intruding on her.

"I want to go home." She fisted her hands.

"I know you do. But it's not going to happen."

"Why?" she demanded. "Why am I here?"

He took the last step, closing the space between them, and grabbed her arms. Giving her a little shake, he said, "Because this is where I want you to be. And that's the only answer you're going to get tonight. You have two options, Azalea. Get undressed and into bed, or you can go over my knee for a punishment."

"Punishment?" She placed her hands flat against his chest, stabilizing herself more than trying to push him away. He had a hard grip; she wasn't getting out of it.

"Disobeying me. That's punishable," he said in a soft voice. "Start as you mean to continue, and I don't allow disobedience, Azalea."

"You kidnapped me," she said. He couldn't possibly think she'd simply go along with him. She needed to get away. She needed to get home.

"You aren't a prisoner here," he said, as though that one sentence cleared up everything.

"But you're going to punish me?" Her voice cracked. She couldn't decide if she wanted to laugh or cry. The man was deranged.

"Not if you make the right choice, although from what I could make out of your ass on the street, I wouldn't mind taking this dress up again and smacking that round ass of yours a few times."

If he hadn't smiled when he said it, hadn't looked so fucking handsome, she could have thought of a retort.

"Choices, choices."

"Will you let me go home tomorrow?" she asked softly. Maybe if the hope was there, a little carrot dangling before her, she could give in to him a bit easier.

He shook his head, putting out the light peeking from the end of the tunnel.

"I have my reasons, Azalea, but I'm not going to discuss them with you yet. Right now, you need to be a good girl and get in bed."

"I'm not tired. How can I sleep here?" she demanded.

He released her arms, took a step back, and licked his lips. "I can help you sleep, if that's what you need." His stare raked over her body, and she moved back again, knocking herself into the cross.

He laughed and shook his head. "Get in bed, Azalea, before I forget I swore to myself I wouldn't touch you tonight."

"You said this is your room. Where will you sleep?" She inched around him and padded over to the bed, kicking her shoes off.

He studied her quietly. The little tic in his jaw was back, and his lids narrowed more the longer he watched her. She climbed onto the massive bed but didn't slide under the covers. No way could she sleep yet.

"Stay in this room, Azalea. There's a washroom through that door if you need it."

She grabbed a pillow and held it over her stomach, hugging it to herself. He ran his tongue over his bottom lip as though coming to terms with a decision then headed back to the door.

"In the morning. We'll talk in the morning." And before she could respond or register his words, he was gone. She waited for the familiar click of a lock sliding into place.

It never came.

CHAPTER 6

"You can't be serious," Daniel said with disapproval. "She's here? Like in the house? Not the Annex?"

Peter opened his laptop and powered up. "I'm pretty sure I didn't stutter. Yes. She's here. Upstairs in my rooms, probably still sleeping." At least that's where she had been when he left his bedroom that morning. When he'd gone up to bed the night before, she had been asleep, still hugging that damn pillow to her body and sitting up against the headboard.

Peter swung his gaze to Daniel and hardened his jaw. "She is under my protection. If any of the men so much as look at her too long, they answer to me. And she's not in the catalog."

The women of the Annex had choices—they could stay or leave at will. They didn't play or sleep with anyone they didn't agree to, and when they did agree to a contract, they had complete say over the terms. Not a single one of them lived there by force.

"I got it. I don't get it, but I got it." Daniel rubbed the back of his neck. "Santos was pretty freaked after you left last night."

"I'm sure he was." Peter leaned back in his chair. "I don't think his boss took too kindly to coming home and finding her daughter missing."

"His boss isn't coming home for a few more weeks."

"Did you see the paintings in that room? The portraits? I'm assuming those were of her. She looked familiar."

Daniel frowned. "Yeah, I noticed that, too, but I figured we'd seen her at a meeting or something. Maybe she works for one of the families."

"What's her name?"

"Bellatrix Gothel," Daniel said.

Peter tossed the name around in his mind but made no connections. An unusual name. If he'd heard it before, surely, he'd remember.

"I want you to find out what you can about her. I want to know who she works for, and what she does. Santos was more afraid of Azalea being taken than he was of us coming for the money."

"Wouldn't you be afraid if someone came to take Ellie while Ash was away?" Daniel pointed out.

"I'd kill anyone who tried, as would you. But this is different. Azalea wasn't simply up in her room, she was locked up there. There's more going on here, and I want to know what it is. I can't place her, but I know Bellatrix is bad news."

"What are you going to do with the girl?" Daniel asked with a tilt to his lips.

"That's not your concern, asshole." Peter went back to logging onto his computer. "You make sure she doesn't leave the grounds and that she's safe when I'm not with her."

"She can roam the house?" Daniel asked with some surprise.

Peter looked at him over the top of his screen. "She's not a prisoner here, Daniel. She just can't leave the estate. And if she goes outside, I want a man with her. For her safety."

Daniel raised his eyebrows but kept his opinion to himself, for which Peter was grateful. He hadn't figured out what the hell to do with her yet. He only knew he needed her with him at the house.

A knock on the door preceded Johnny entering, a canary-eating grin on his lips. "Your damsel is looking for you." He jerked a thumb at the door.

"His damsel?" Daniel chuckled.

"Yeah, the girl he took last night. The blond."

Peter's stomach twisted. "Her name is Azalea," he ground out. They weren't acting any different than any other day, but they were talking about Azalea—not some girl off the street looking for a payday.

Johnny straightened out his smile. "Right. Sorry. Azalea is looking for you. I showed her to the kitchen and asked Maria to make her something to eat then said I'd get you."

Peter waved him off. "Fine. I'll be there in a minute. Go find something else to do."

"One more thing," Johnny said. "Aubree stumbled in at two in the morning, piss drunk."

"So?" The girls were free to come and go as they wished. If she went and had a bit of fun, that was her business.

"She hadn't checked out before she left. No one knew where she was until she came home," Johnny finished explaining.

Peter blew out a breath. He had enough to deal with at the moment, and handing this little problem to an employee was tempting. "Fine. I'll meet with her this afternoon. Let her sleep it off." He closed the laptop, giving up on getting any research done. "Daniel, go away. You're annoying the fuck out of me this morning."

"I didn't do anything yet."

"Exactly. Go get some work done." Peter walked out of the office.

☙ ☙ ☙

Peter found Azalea sitting at the small breakfast table in the kitchen, a steaming cup of coffee nestled between her slender hands. She stared out the large windows into the gardens in the back. Not wanting to disturb her yet, he gave a small nod to Maria, excusing her from the kitchen.

Maria had been working for the Titon family since he could remember, and it didn't take any more than the small gesture for her to get moving. She gave one cursory look toward Azalea before leaving, letting him know in her own way that she had concerns about the situation. She may worry, but she wouldn't vocalize her doubts, or get involved.

Once the kitchen cleared, Peter cleared his throat softly, nudging Azalea out of whatever thoughts she'd lost herself in. She turned toward him. Her body stiffened the moment she faced him.

"Good morning," he offered gently.

"Morning," she replied and brought her cup to her lips. She'd combed her hair before coming down, but she still had the freshly woken look about her. A small crease from the pillowcase embellished her left cheek.

When he'd found her sitting up the night before, he'd maneuvered her under the covers and gotten her comfortable before climbing in with her.

"Did you eat something? I can have Maria make you eggs if you want, waffles, maybe?"

"I'm fine," she said flatly, taking another sip of coffee.

Peter poured himself a cup and joined her at the table. Soft beams of sunlight streaming through the frosted windows cast an angelic glow around Azalea.

"Sleep okay?"

"No."

"You looked pretty damn peaceful." He kept his irritation mostly in check, but he didn't like being ignored, and she was doing her best to make him feel cast aside.

"You checked on me?" Her large eyes moved up from her coffee to him.

"I slept right beside you." Ah, there it was. The little flash of surprise. "How do you think you got under the covers?"

"I—" She snapped her mouth closed. "Will you be taking me home today?"

"We covered that topic pretty thoroughly last night. You aren't going home."

"You said we would talk," she pointed out.

He sipped his coffee. Maria had used the dark roast.

"I did say that."

"So—talk," she urged him.

"I expected less attitude from you this morning."

"You'll have to forgive me. I'm new to this whole abduction thing." She grabbed her cup, spilling a drop onto the table before bringing the mug to her lips.

"Tell me about your mother." He decided to ignore her jab. If she wanted to talk, he had a few questions.

"What about her? She's a mother." Azalea faced him.

"What sort of work does she do? Your father? How about him?" He didn't recall seeing any pictures of a man in the library there.

"She's in sales or something. I'm not entirely sure." Azalea's voice softened. "She's going to be very upset if I'm not there when she gets home. You don't understand." The same sense of urgency laced her words as the night he'd driven her home from Tower.

"Any mother would be upset—"

"No! You don't understand. If she finds out you took me, if she finds out I'm not home—" She lowered her head.

"She'll blame you?"

"Just let me go home."

"That's not happening. Tell me more about her. Why lock you in your room?"

"It was for safety," she said with gritted teeth. "Do you think you saved me from something? Because you didn't. You've made it worse."

"Made what worse? You're talking in circles." Peter leaned forward, ignoring his coffee. "I want a straight answer. Why were you locked in your room?"

She took a deep breath. "My mother lost a daughter before I was born. She was kidnapped and never found. So, my mother is a little overprotective. Scared it will happen again."

"You're not a child. And your door was locked from the outside. Keeping you in, not people out," Peter pointed out.

Azalea rubbed her forehead. "She wants to be sure I don't get hurt."

He could piece together the truth of it. Azalea didn't want to be stuck inside, so she'd go out, and to be sure she didn't stray from the house, she was locked in.

"And your father?"

"I don't know. I don't remember him, and Mother doesn't talk of him."

He hadn't had the most traditional family growing up, but he remembered both of his parents. Knew what lengths a parent would go to to protect their child, but still, he couldn't see either of them locking him away in the name of safety.

"And Richard Santos?"

Azalea put her head back and let out a groan. "He works for my mother, keeps the house safe. Now, you answer me. Why did you take me? If Santos owes money, my mother will pay it for him."

"You're here because I want you here. That's all you need to know."

"You talk about my mother with contempt, as if her keeping me safe is some unthinkable crime. But, you're the same. You didn't lock the bedroom door, but I bet if I walk out the front door, your men will stop me. I'm just as much locked in here as I was there. And you'll say it's for my safety." She pushed the cup away and stood from the chair.

"I'm sure it seems the same to you, but it isn't." He couldn't offer any more than that, seeing as he was acting purely on gut instinct.

"I want to go home." She slammed her open palm on the table, knocking over her mug. What little coffee was left spilled.

He stood and walked around the table until his chest was butted up against her shoulder. Snaking his hand beneath her long hair, he fisted it and pulled her head back, eliciting a soft yelp.

Bringing his mouth to her ear, he inhaled her scent.

"Temper tantrums don't work for me. Clean up the mess you made." He shoved her forward until her mouth hovered over the spillage.

"I hate you," she said in a harsh whisper.

"That's fine with me. Now, clean it."

Her hands flailed behind her, trying to get hold of him, but he snatched up the closest one and pinned it to her back, forcing her to use the other to steady herself over the table.

"Your tongue, Azalea. Clean it up with your tongue."

She stomped a foot, but it made no difference. She

wouldn't be getting back up until every drop of the coffee was clean and she understood who held the power.

After a long pause, her little pink tongue slipped out, and she ran it over the droplets. It took several licks to clean the area, and by the time she finished, his cock was as hard as the granite tiling of the floor they stood on. It was supposed to be punishment, but she made it as seductive as a striptease—and probably didn't even know it.

"Good girl." He pulled her back upright and used his thumb to wipe a bit of coffee from her chin.

She pinched her lips together but didn't say a word. She didn't need to, he knew anger when he saw it. But he also knew arousal when he saw it, and her eyes were as dilated as they had been at Tower when she'd watched him whip Cassandra.

"I don't want to hear another word about going home. If you bring it up one more time, you'll be punished."

"Some hero you are," she ground out.

He chuckled and pressed his lips to her cheek. "I never claimed to be a hero, but I'm not the villain here, either. Now, I have to see to some business. I've had a few dresses brought to our room. Shower and put one on. Either stay upstairs, or you can explore the estate. You may not leave. There will be men with you if you go outside, but you may wander the gardens as much as you want. The Annex is off-limits until I can give you the tour myself. Do you think you can handle that?"

"Yes." She spat the word. He didn't miss her fisted hands or how tight her jaw clenched, but he wasn't going to console her yet. The sooner she understood the dynamic, the sooner she'd relax into her new home.

He let go of her hair and smoothed it before stepping away from her. "I know you're confused, and when I'm ready, I'll explain everything. For the time being, you're going to have to trust me."

"Because so far, you've given off that trustworthy vibe." She folded her arms over her chest, covering her breasts but also pulling the neckline of her dress down enough to give him a peek at the swollen mounds beneath.

"I suggest you start controlling the sarcasm and snark, or I'll do it for you." He touched the buckle of his belt, and grinned when her eyes widened. If he touched her, he had no doubt he'd find her wet and wanting, but he wouldn't. Not yet. Soon.

"More threats."

"I don't threaten. I mean what I say. Always." He lived by his word. His father had embedded that into him from a young age. Never threaten, always deliver, and mean everything you promise. His father had lived by that, and Peter would do the same.

"Don't you have work to do?" she asked, taking some of the bite out of her tone.

He watched her silently then backed away from her. "Go on." He waved her off.

Watching her leave the kitchen with her back tense, her hands fisting at her sides, made his own muscles lock up, but he wouldn't go after her. He'd let her stew for a little while longer. Once he had more answers, when he could start piecing the faded memories together then he could tell her everything.

But not until then.

Until then, she'd learn to follow his lead. She'd obey him, or she'd face the consequences.

CHAPTER 7

The damn dress fit too snug. Azalea pulled at the hem again. She didn't like having such tight-fitting clothing. She wanted her cotton dress back. Or some yoga pants. Anything that would cover more of her body.

Where the hell had he gotten these dresses?

Azalea made her way down the staircase to the main floor of the house. She kept herself tucked away all morning and needed to get out of the room. His room. Where everything smelled like him and reminded her of him.

He'd slept with her. She didn't remember him climbing into bed, but she also didn't remember falling asleep. The last memory she had of the night before was holding the pillow against her and planning to get up and find a way out of the house as soon as enough time passed from his leaving her.

Peter told her if she went outside someone would be with her, but she didn't see anyone when she stepped onto the bottom landing. No men guarded the front door, and she couldn't see anyone in the large living room right off the stairwell.

She made her way to the front door, thankful her soft-soled shoes didn't make any sound. After another look around and assuring herself she was indeed alone, she grasped the knob and sighed happily when she found it turning with ease.

The door opened silently, and she squeezed through a small opening and gently pulled it closed behind her. It had been dark when Peter drove her up to the house the night before, but she had a good sense of where she was. She needed to get outside the gates then down the hill to town. Once there, she could grab a cab home. Santos would pay the driver once she was there.

But first, she needed to get through the gate. All she could do was hope the mammoth from the night before wasn't there. Unless she could find another way through. If he was there and she had to abort her attempt, she'd at least learn a bit more of the layout. She'd been sneaking out of her own house for many years; she could manage to get out of this place.

She slowed and tried to see through the slim windows of the security house. If the mammoth was in there, he was hiding pretty well. The next thing she'd need was to get inside the building and find the mechanism because she doubted the wrought iron gates would open manually.

Shielding her eyes from the bright afternoon sun, she checked the guard house again. Still no movement. Maybe it was only manned while Peter was away.

The door to the guard house was unlocked, and she made quick work of getting inside. She found the switch easily enough and reached for it.

But before she touched anything, she could hear the subtle creak of the iron moving.

Peter hadn't mentioned leaving, but he hadn't told her anything except he had work to do. Maybe it was just a visitor. She could still get out, get away from the house.

Pressing against the wall, out of sight through the window, she held her breath, waiting for the vehicle to pull through and continue up the drive.

Nothing.

Was it idling at the entrance?

A car door slammed, and heavy footsteps made their way to her hiding spot. She squeezed her eyes closed and turned her head away from the door.

A deep chuckle blasted through the silence.

"Azalea."

She willed the voice to go away.

"Azalea, I can see you. Closing your eyes doesn't make me actually go away." Peter's levity made her heart stop pounding or the hairs on the back of her neck stop standing on end.

Realizing she'd moved up to her toes in an effort to completely flatten herself against the wall, she lowered herself and opened her eyes. Peter hadn't come inside; he was leaning through the open window.

"You were trying to run away again." He pushed the door open and walked through.

"I—" There wasn't much sense in lying, since he'd caught her. "What did you expect me to do?" she asked instead.

"I expected you to stay on the grounds like I told you to. I expected you to have more sense than to use the front entrance as a way of escape."

He wasn't wearing his suit. A simple buttoned-down white shirt tucked neatly into black slacks held up with a thick, worn, black leather belt. She could make out some of his tattoos through the thin material of his sleeves.

"If you hadn't come home just now, it would have worked." She thrust her chin up. Given the darkening of his scowl after she spoke, it probably wasn't the best time to proclaim such a small victory.

"Did you honestly think I didn't have men watching you? Did you really think you'd merely open the gates and walk out of here?" His voice deepened, sending a chill up her spine. The levity disappeared.

"I—" She snapped her mouth shut. She hadn't seen anyone, but that didn't mean they weren't there. "So, one of your men called you? Tattled on me?"

"I gave you freedom of the house, the yards, everywhere, and still you try to leave?"

"You are so stupid!" she yelled. The events of the past day were too much. All of it had worn her down. "You can't kidnap a woman and expect her to simply fall in line! I won't stop trying to leave. I won't stop trying to get home! You can't keep me!" She lunged at him, shoving at his chest and trying to make it out the door.

His thick arm wrapped easily around her throat, yanking her backward until she crashed into his massive chest. Breath couldn't come fast enough, her lungs heaved for air.

But not him.

He simply held her, his breathing easy and soft against her ear.

"That's enough." His dark tenor washed over her, sucking the fight out of her. She dropped her hands to her sides and took a slow, ragged breath.

"Please…let me go," she pleaded on a whisper.

"Never." A solid statement. "Now, since you've proven you can't follow directions, and you've promised to keep trying to escape, I'll have to make other arrangements for you."

"What? No. I'll—" Her words were cut off by the clamp of his hand over her mouth. She sucked in air through her nose, struggling to get enough, but he didn't budge.

"No more talking. You've said enough, Azalea." He pushed her forward, frog walking her outside the guard house. He didn't turn to the car, still idling just inside the gates, but shoved her toward the house.

She managed to keep up with his pace, not that she had a choice with his arm around her chest and his hand cutting off most of her air.

When they got to the stairs, he released her, spun her, and threw her over his shoulder. Her stomach lurched when it landed across his muscular build.

"Peter—"

A sharp smack to her bottom stilled her. "I said enough. Don't make it worse." His voice, though still velvety smooth, held a darker quality.

The door opened to the house, and the bright light of the afternoon quickly dissipated to darkness. Looking up as best she could, she saw another man—one who had been with Peter at her house the night before—standing at the door.

"No one comes upstairs," Peter said as he walked through the foyer and ascended the staircase. Each step made her bounce on his shoulder.

He was taking her up to his room. He'd lock her in for sure this time. She'd tried to escape too soon. She should have taken the time to learn the layout of the house, figured out where his men were, and maneuvered around them. Exactly like at home.

Instead, she'd seen an opportunity and run with it. Like an idiot.

And now he'd lock her away.

When they reached his suite, he didn't stop at his bedroom. He went to another door and opened it, walking into a darkened area. He spun around, shutting and bolting the door. Her head swam from all the movements and dangling upside down.

He bent forward, bringing her to her feet. She wiped the hair from her face and took a small step to get her bearings.

"Strip."

The hard command surprised her.

She tucked her long strands of hair behind her ears and peered up at him. He had to be joking. He was trying to scare her.

His narrowed eyes, tense jaw, and stern expression didn't imply any sort of amusement.

"Why?"

"Three seconds before I do it for you." He lifted three fingers in the air. "One." He lowered one finger.

"Wait. No. Okay." She waved at him and retreated backward.

"Two." Another finger bent.

"No." She shook her head and looked around for somewhere to hide, to put distance between them.

Someone could have hit her in the chest, and it would have felt better than the shock at what she saw before her.

A human-sized cage. Taller than her, and wide enough for several people to stand inside together. Beside the cage, another spanking bench, like the one in his room. The wall was covered with hooks. Implements hung from half of them. Paddles, whips, floggers, leather straps—things she'd seen online but never in real life. They looked so much worse in real life.

"Three."

She tried to run away, but he gripped her shoulders, spinning her to face him. With one tug at the neckline, he tore her dress. The dress split down the middle, and he ripped the flimsy material until it hung from her arms.

"You monster." She tried to cover herself, but he smacked away her hands and finished pulling the clothing off her body then reached for her bra.

"No. I will. Just stop!" She jumped back, trying to whack him away.

She kept her gaze off him, not wanting to see his anger, and reached behind her to unclasp her bra. The white cotton slid down her arms, freeing her breasts as the cups dropped. She tossed it to the floor, onto the ruined and discarded dress, pushed her panties over her hips, and kicked them to join the others.

Instinctively, she wrapped one arm over her breasts, and pressed an open hand to her groin, trying to reclaim some dignity.

"Look at me," he ordered, and not wanting to give him reason to do anything else to her, she did.

The anger she assumed would be raging in his expression wasn't there. The dark storm still lingered, but he wasn't out of control with rage.

She would have been more comfortable with anger than his calm disapproval. Did he ever lose control?

"Drop your hands to your sides." The next order was given.

She released her breasts but pulled her hair forward, thankful the long locks were able to give her some cover then let both arms dangle at her sides.

He made a slow appraisal of her naked form. A grin eased onto his lips when he finally reached her eyes.

"Get on the bench, grab the handles, and put your ass high in the air," he instructed, reaching for his belt buckle.

"No." She shook her head. She would not give in so easily.

"No?" He quirked an eyebrow. "Did you just say no?"

"That's what I said." She made fists to keep from trying to cover her body again. She would not give him weakness. The monster probably fed off it, and she would rather see him starved.

He dropped his hands, the belt already unbuckled and hanging open at his waist. "Okay." He nodded.

Her stomach twisted. That wasn't a good okay. That was definitely an, *I'll think of something worse* okay.

With two large strides, he grabbed her arms, pulled her to the cage. She struggled, yanking back and cursing at him—not that she expected any of it to work, but she wouldn't go willingly into the prison.

He didn't open the door. Instead, he reached up and pulled down a pair of cuffs from the top. He shoved her forward until her body was pressed against the long black bars. Her hands were drawn up over her head. Her struggles were no match for his strength, and she found her wrists bound in the cuffs.

Without the use of her upper body, she kicked out with her feet.

"Can't forget those," he said almost lightheartedly.

One ankle then the other was grasped and pulled out and locked in another set of cuffs until she was completely stretched out against the cage.

She pulled hard, but nothing would give. Completely naked, exposed, her backside faced him.

The jangling of his buckle reminded her of his mission, and her ass clenched in response.

"No. Peter. Please," she begged, trying to turn her head to see him, to plead with him. "Don't do this."

"This was your decision, Azalea. You would have gotten a few licks of my belt on the bench, but now—now you're getting a true strapping."

His fingertips ran over her smooth buttocks, and she tried to jerk to the side, but he had her completely trapped.

Panic rose in her chest. "I'm sorry I tried to run away," she said at the sound of his leather belt rubbing against the loops of his pants as he pulled it free.

"I'm glad you are, but that doesn't change the consequences. See, being sorry afterward and facing no punishment won't get it in your head not to do it again. So, it's my job to be sure you learn this lesson." He palmed her right ass cheek. "I mean really learn it."

"Don't do this. Please." She tugged again on the restraints.

"You did this, Azalea. This is all because of your choices." His hand left her ass, but only for a moment. It made contact. Hard, sharp pain radiated through her once then twice before he moved to her left cheek and repeated the action.

She squeezed her eyelids closed when his hand ran along her shoulder blades, gathering her hair and pushing it forward until her back was completely exposed. The long tendrils reached her bottom when she leaned her head back; at least he moved them out of the way. But was it an action to keep her hair from being pulled, or to make his target more accessible.

The first lash of the leather crossed her ass, bringing with it a white-hot fire she'd never experienced. It took her breath away. She sucked in air just as the second lash hit its target.

She screamed.

Another lash and another.

"Stop!" she cried out, twisting to avoid the strikes but failing miserably.

"Not yet," he announced and continued to administer the punishment.

He didn't leave an inch of her ass unmarked as he brought the length of his belt down on her over and over again, moving up and down her bottom. She screeched when the leather landed on her thighs.

"Please! I'm sorry!" she cried, tears rolling uncontrolled down her cheeks. Pain, unadulterated pain coursed through her bottom as he continued.

"Almost done," he promised in a soft voice. How the hell could he be so calm while delivering such a harsh spanking?

"I can't—please—no more!" She yanked hard on the cuffs.

She could take the rest, and she would, but her mind was reeling from the sharpness of each strike.

His response was to move his mark higher, onto the fleshy part of her ass. She must be a bright-red mess.

All she'd had to do was stay on the estate. That was all he'd asked. He'd given her free rein of the house, aside from the one wing he wanted to escort her through. But she'd tried to run. Until this moment, he hadn't hurt her, hadn't done anything to make her fear him, but she'd gone against him anyway.

Any reasonable person would try to escape. But he'd warned her. He'd told her what would happen, and now she hung from a cage, her ass being blistered by his belt.

He'd kept his word.

"I won't run again!" she called out, meaning it, knowing she would never make another attempt. Not if being caught would bring this hellhound to her door.

He paused.

"I swear it, Peter. I won't," she huffed, sucking in air, feeling the burn of her throat from her cries, the ache in her chest from lack of breath.

"It's not safe for you to run off." The tips of his fingers ran along her ass, making her hiss from the tenderness. She imagined how swollen her cheeks were, how red and bruised.

"It's not safe for me here," she whispered, pressing her forehead against the bars and letting the tears dry on her cheeks.

"I know you're confused. I know this is all probably pretty scary, but all you can do is focus on what I tell you." He crushed his body against hers, his hard length pressing against her naked ass.

"How is being locked in here better than being locked in

at home?" she asked quietly. Would she ever find the freedom she sought?

"You aren't locked in here, Azalea. And if you follow my rules, if you behave, you won't feel the sting of my belt again." He ground his hips into her ass, making her too aware of his cock pushing against her.

"When you're a good girl, when you listen, you'll have so much pleasure. So much happiness, you'll wonder why you ever wanted to run away." His lips brushed against her ear.

"You're insane." She forced a hardness to her words, but she could admit at least to herself that, through the burn of her ass, she sensed the rising arousal in her belly. Her pussy was wet. From the first lash to the last, she'd felt her body responding to his harshness.

He knew it, too.

Fingers slipped between her ass cheeks, pressing against her puckered hole then moved lower until he found the wetness she couldn't stop.

"Ah, there you are." He kissed the spot behind her ear. "There's the Azalea I met at Tower. The woman turned on by a whipping, the woman fighting her own desires, her own sexuality." He rolled his finger over her sensitive clit, now swollen and wanting from her punishment.

"No." She tried to shake her head, to deny what he said, but he kissed her cheek.

"I don't like that word from you. I should forbid you to use it." He pinched her clit, sending a wave of electricity through her body.

All her strength had been used during the belting, so she couldn't stop the moan of pleasure escaping her lips when he pinched again.

"Imagine how quickly you'd come for me if I thrust my cock in you, or if I sucked on this little clit of yours." He slid his fingers back, circling her entrance. "How fast will you come unglued for me if I fuck you with my fingers?"

Heaven help her, if he didn't stop talking, she'd come purely from his voice.

"But, you were a very naughty girl, and you can't have an orgasm yet." He pulled away, all touch evaporated from her, leaving her burning for an entirely different reason.

The pain of her ass made itself known again as the ache in her pussy ebbed. She dropped her head, wanting to cry, for the loss of her dignity, for the loss of any hope at freedom, and for the loss of his touch.

He released her ankles from the cuffs and wrapped an arm around her waist while uncuffing her wrists.

"I won't lock you in here," he said picking her up in his arms, but not being at all careful of the soreness in her ass as he did so. "Unless you make me. If you run again, I will," he promised.

He carried her into his bedroom again with her arms wrapped around his neck and her head resting against his chest.

His aftershave smelled good. Like something she could snuggle into.

Peter placed her on the bed, ass down, and grinned at her when she winced from the fabric rubbing her skin.

"I won't lock you in, but I am going to put a man outside the door." He leaned over her face, ran his fingers over the streaks of dried tears. "One of my men will escort you when you leave this room. No more bad behavior, Azalea." He touched the tip of her nose.

"When will this end?" she asked softly, watching his lips.

"I can't tell you that."

"Can't or won't?"

He remained silent for a long moment then brought his mouth over hers. She should have fought it, turned her head and denied him, but instead she sank into the warmth of his touch.

When his tongue pushed between her lips, she danced with it, taking the kiss deeper, wanting more than just his mouth on her.

He ended the kiss abruptly and pressed one warm peck to her cheek. "Sleep for now."

"Are you going to leave me more clothes? The dresses you brought up are a little tight," she said.

He stood from the bed. "No. No clothes."

"What?" She sat up.

He opened the door and grinned back at her. "Naked women are less likely to try to escape."

"But you said I could leave the room, that your men will be out there."

He nodded. "And they will. You are free to roam the estate, Azalea."

She threw a pillow, but the door closed behind him before it reached him.

He had stuck to his word. He didn't lock the door. She was free to walk around as much as she wanted.

Completely naked.

He'd still found a way to keep her trapped.

CHAPTER 8

Peter found Daniel and Johnny in the Annex. There wouldn't be another catalog party until Ash returned from his honeymoon, but there were still daily events happening. The girls had appointments and clients to entertain.

"I want two men stationed on my floor. One of them right outside my bedroom. I want another one at the bottom of the staircase. If Azalea comes down, I want someone with her at all times, and I'm to be notified." Peter pointed a long finger at Daniel. "And I want someone at the goddamn gate until I have this all situated."

"The gate?" Daniel's eyebrows rose. "Sure, I'll get Tommy on it. Something happen?"

Peter ran his hand across the back of his neck. "Azalea was trying to open the gates when I got back from checking in at Tower. If I hadn't come home when I did, she'd be halfway to town." The little flash of her hair in the window had given her away in the guard house. If he hadn't been leaning out of his car to punch in his code, he probably would have missed it. She wouldn't have had to flick the switch to open the gates; he would have helped her right along.

"Shit." Daniel turned to Johnny. "Didn't you put a man out there?"

"Yeah, in the gardens. You said she had the run of the house."

"I don't want her off the estate," Peter stated. He should have informed the men he wanted more guards on her, wanted eyes on her while she was on the grounds. Catching her had been pure luck, but he would be more prepared in the future.

"What's happening here?" Peter turned the topic to business. After spending the last half hour with Azalea, his cock needed the distraction.

"Amber and Annie have play sessions this afternoon, and Aubree's off duty until you deal with her," Daniel said.

Aubree. Right. Peter let out a heavy sigh. Dealing with errant women in the Annex had always given him a thrill. He enjoyed his job as disciplinarian of the house. But at the moment, it seemed more of a chore than a joy.

"She'll keep," Peter said. "What about the other girls? Are we having a slow week? Only two girls have play sessions?"

"I think some of the others are taking time off. You know, with Ash gone—"

"Cat's away so mice play, that shit? Make sure we have enough girls on duty to handle the regulars. The others can take off. But make certain they actually take the time off. I want them listed as off duty, not just declining appointments." Like any other place of employment, vacation was part of the benefit package, but Peter wouldn't allow the girls to merely take undocumented days off.

"You got it." Johnny nodded.

"What about Tower?" Daniel asked. "Do any of the girls there want to take a day here?"

Peter shook his head. "The two businesses stay separate. If they want to, they'll have to come apply on their own. I won't shift girls from here to there or there to here." Peter had opened Tower on his own. It was not a Titon business, and it would remain completely independent of that brand.

"Are you going there tonight?" Daniel asked.

"Not sure yet." Peter didn't mention it depended completely on the behavior and attitude of the beautiful, naughty blond upstairs in his room. "What did you find out about Santos and Bellatrix?"

Johnny answered. "Santos is gone. Azalea's house is empty. The other men who were staying there are gone, too. I think they're spooked that their boss's daughter was taken and they didn't stop it."

"I have a few feelers out about Bellatrix. So far, no one's talking, but if she's working with any of the families—and from the look of that house and how scared those men were, I'd say she has connections in some pretty high places—we'll find something," Daniel added.

"I want Santos found, and I want him brought here. I have questions for him." Peter's jaw ached from the tension the thought of the prick brought to him.

"We'll find him," Daniel promised.

"Maybe she worked with Samuel. Any chance she would be listed in one of those old records?" Johnny offered.

Peter shook his head. "What sort of accurate records do you think Samuel kept while he was kidnapping and selling women?"

"I'm just sayin', he did keep some records. Maybe she's in there if she worked with the families in the past. Maybe she worked with him."

Not a bad point.

"The old record books are downstairs. Go through them, and let me know if you find anything. But Samuel used codes, too, so you can play super sleuth for a little while."

"No problem." Johnny grinned. He probably felt more powerful being given a job. Everyone worked their way up the ranks, legit business or not, and the Titon family wasn't any different. Johnny was making his way.

"Why's this woman so interesting to you, anyway?" Daniel probed. "I never even heard of her until the other night when we grabbed her daughter. Which brings me to the second question. Why did we grab Azalea?"

Peter narrowed his gaze. His motives weren't up for discussion, and they sure as hell weren't up for judgment from his men.

"My reasons are my business. Keeping this place running and safe is your business. Now, get to work." Peter turned on his heel and made his way back to the main house. He wouldn't explain his reasoning to the men on any given day, but at the moment, even if he wanted to, he couldn't. He didn't understand his actions any more than they did. He knew he had to get Azalea out of that house, and he could feel in his bones something wasn't right with her mother.

"Peter?" a soft voice called to him before he reached the door.

"Aubree. You're supposed to be in your apartment until I call for you." He turned to face her. She had both hands clasped in front of her, and her hair had been straightened and laid flat over her shoulders. With a pink tint to her cheeks, she looked almost virginal.

"I know. It's just I really need the extra shift at Sampson's or Delilah's, and Daniel said I can't take any work until you've—well, until we've talked."

"You should have considered that before you broke the house rules," he said, folding his arms over his chest. Showing her any empathy would give her false hope.

"I'm sorry." Her shoulders dropped, but her stare remained fixated on his boot.

"We'll talk tonight. You'll be back on the roster tomorrow," he said in a flat voice, and left her in the hall. Aubree wasn't a timid woman. He had interviewed her himself, and she'd been outspoken and had a strong resolve. This wouldn't be the first time he took his belt to her for disobeying a house rule. It probably wouldn't be the last, either. Why would she not sign out when she went out for the evening? It boggled him why some of the girls would put their asses on the line over such easy-to-follow rules.

But he already had one female he didn't quite understand, and he didn't have time to figure out this puzzle as well. He'd deal with her later.

Peter walked through the living room and headed for the staircase.

"Uh, your—well—the girl is in the kitchen." Jacob stopped him before he went up.

Peter looked down the corridor leading to the kitchen. "Azalea?"

"Yeah. She wanted something to eat. Tommy said she could roam the house," he qualified quickly.

Peter stalked off to the kitchen. She had already proven herself stubborn, but did she really leave his room and stride down to the kitchen naked? How many of the men had seen?

He threw open the swing door and barged into the kitchen, expecting to see a gloating woman standing in the center of the room with her hand perched on her naked hip.

"I couldn't find bread." Azalea looked up from the kitchen island where she rolled a slice of ham. No smugness. No nudeness, either.

She'd taken the sheet from his bed and fashioned a toga-style dress.

Fighting back the lift of his lips, he strolled to the pantry.

He slid a panel open and pulled out a loaf of honey-wheat bread.

"Oh. I didn't see that." She slid the rolled ham into her mouth.

"I remember telling you no clothing." He pushed the loaf toward her on the island, stepping around it to get a better look at her.

She shrugged. "This isn't clothing. This is a sheet." She rolled another piece of ham, apparently no longer interested in making a sandwich.

He plucked the meat from her fingers, drawing her gaze to him. "Clever girl." He ran his thumb over her jawline then down her neck until he reached the sheet.

Her stare didn't waver. She wouldn't pull away from him, no matter how much she wanted to. And he could see that battle in her. She hadn't learned to mask as much emotion as she thought she had. She liked his touch, but fought against the desire.

"Are you going to punish me again?" The question was asked in a low, husky tone.

"Do you want me to?" He searched her eyes while caressing the knot of the sheet on her shoulder. One tug, and he'd have her naked again. Only this time, he wasn't rushed, he'd enjoy the view for as long as he liked. He'd inspect every curve, every freckle, every inch of her before he allowed her to dress again.

"You know what I want." She pressed her shoulders back, trying to put on a brave face.

"I know what you *say* you want." He slipped a digit beneath the sheet, trailing it down from the knot to the top of her breast.

"I'm not as naive as you think I am. I know what you do for a living. I know how you and your cousin make all your money. You sell sex. You sell women, and when you aren't doing that, you prey on the weak who come looking for help."

Peter paused and dragged his attention from her breasts to her eyes. Her hardening nipples didn't go unnoticed. Nor her attempt to deflect the moment by switching gears.

"Not naive, but definitely misinformed. And I'm not discussing family business with you." He slipped his hand into the sheet until he reached her nipple. Taking it between two fingers, he squeezed.

She gasped and tried to jerk back. He didn't let go. She brought her hand up, covering his, trying to draw him away from her.

"I'm not letting go until I want to," he said, intensifying his grip. "It would greatly benefit you to learn quickly who is in charge here, who asks the questions, who sets the rules, and who allows whom to come and go. You see, it doesn't matter what you want, it matters what I want."

She winced but stopped her attempt to still him.

He waited until her shimmering eyes met his. Tears, that didn't fall, perched on her lids.

He released her. She quickly sucked in a breath and clamped her arm over her breast. The sting would be short-lived, but it would be intense as the blood rushed back to her pert nipple.

"If I slip my finger through your pussy lips, will I find them wet?" he asked. She jerked her body farther away from him. He chuckled. "I think I have my answer."

"Asshole," she muttered under her breath, still clutching her chest.

"Guilty." He grinned at her. Seeing the mixture of arousal and fear in her eyes made his cock hard. If she were on her knees giving him the same look, he'd probably lose his load.

"But I didn't come in here to argue with you." He sighed, pushing the loaf of bread closer to her and giving her space by walking around the island. "I have to work tonight. You'll be coming with me."

"Why?"

"Mostly because I want you to, but also, you didn't get a chance to see much at Tower during your last visit. I thought you might enjoy exploring instead of sitting in my room." And he wouldn't be leaving her behind at the house to snoop around for an escape.

"Will I be going naked?" she shot at him.

He laughed again. Such fire from a woman who he had no doubt had spent most of her existence being locked away from life.

"Depends on you." He said nothing more. Let her figure out what she needed to do in order to get clothing. She didn't know that there was no fucking way he'd be letting her walk around Tower nude. No one would set their eyes on her naked form until he had a chance to truly see her.

No one.

CHAPTER 9

The noise of the club didn't drown out the thudding of Azalea's heart in her ears. The pounding of the music, the swell of the people dancing, the laughter rising and falling around her kicked up her anxiety.

She'd been in the middle of all the crowd days before, yet this time, she couldn't get her heart rate to calm, or her breath to catch.

Maybe it was the form-fitting black dress with the plunging neckline and nonexistent back that Peter had given her to wear. Or perhaps the way the men all but licked their lips when she walked through the crowd, behind Peter. He'd given some protection—no one would dare mess with him—but once he passed the men, their stares went straight to her. She gripped Peter's hand harder as they made their way to his office.

Once they were in the back of the club, out of the crowd, she felt the breath come back to her lungs. Peter paused, turning to her with concern.

"There're more people than before," she said lamely.

"You don't like crowds?" he asked, running his thumb

over her knuckles. She hadn't let go of him, and she wasn't quite ready to.

"I'm not used to them. The music wasn't as loud before, either." She placed her free hand over her chest, trying to gain control over herself again.

"We reach capacity nearly every night. Maybe tonight's different for another reason." He pushed a loose strand of hair from her face.

She swallowed hard and let go of his hand. His lips curled into a smile, but he didn't reach for her again.

"You sure bringing me here was a good idea? I mean, there's a lot of people. I could ask for help, get lost in the crowd, and slip out onto the street." All possibilities she'd already run through her head but knew wouldn't work. He had too many men, and she didn't know who or where they were.

"Yeah, there are probably at least a dozen ways for you to get away tonight. But, you won't. Because you know you'll be caught, and you know what happens when you get caught." He reached around her and grabbed her ass. She clenched her teeth together at the soreness, but she would not show him her discomfort.

After he'd given her the dress along with the order to get ready for a night out, she'd examined her backside in the mirror. Three bruises had already formed on her cheeks. She wasn't looking to add to them. He had that much right.

"I think you like beating women," she shot at him. Getting that handsome confident grin off his face became a priority. Being attracted to him needed to stop, and the more he gave her his half smile, the more that little crease on his left cheek popped up, the more she wanted to have his lips on her again.

He chuckled at her accusation. "I don't beat them. But I

do enjoy disciplining a naughty submissive. It rights the ship, if you know what I mean."

"No. I don't know what that means," she argued, knowing exactly what he was talking about. After he'd strapped her and put her to bed, she'd had plenty of time to get her head wrapped around the incident. When she should have been angry and plotting revenge, she had been calm and aroused. The strapping had hurt, and she would feel it at least for the rest of the day, but Peter hadn't been overly cruel. In fact, it was his darkness that drew her to him. The confident way he simply took control and gave her no leniency for what she'd done.

But she wouldn't admit any of that to him. No. She may have felt calm settle over her after he strapped her, but she knew it was wrong. She should want him dead for touching her. She should want to kill him herself for the hungry way he kept looking at her.

She should.

But she didn't.

Peter leaned in closer to her, caressing her cheek. "Such a stubborn girl." He patted her. "But I know how to deal with that."

She forced herself to pull away from his touch, and received a laugh from him for her effort.

"I need to see to a few things. You have a choice here, Azalea. You can sit in my private box to the left of the main stage and listen to the music and watch the show about to start, or you can sit in my office with me."

The change in his voice when he offered the second choice made her believe watching him work would be exactly that. Sitting and watching. Sitting in his private box would give her the ability to see the show, to see how the other couples in the club reacted and played. She'd get to see exactly what she'd wanted to the first night she'd come.

And he knew it. She could sense it even if he wouldn't admit to it.

"I'll sit in your box," she answered with a soft tone. He was offering a short olive branch. Very short, considering she still wasn't able to walk out and go home, but at least he wasn't shackling her to him.

"Sergio will be standing by. Anything you need, just ask him." Peter gestured to the side, and a man stepped out of the shadows. The mammoth from the guard building.

"I thought you said you keep your business separate from the Titon ones?" she asked, eying the large man walking up to them. If his sheer size didn't keep people away, his fierce scowl would do the job perfectly fine.

"I do. When I stay at the house, Sergio comes with. He's part of my personal security team." Peter turned to the man in question. "She's not to leave the box unescorted for any reason. Have a bottle of wine brought to her table and a bread and cheese platter. She didn't eat very much dinner."

"*She* is right here, and *she* isn't very hungry," Azalea said.

"I'll be in my office but will join her shortly." Peter continued to address the mammoth.

Azalea rolled her eyes.

"Yes, sir." Sergio turned his attention to Azalea. "After you." He gestured for her to walk back down the hall she'd just entered.

"Azalea." Peter's hard tone stopped her a few paces in. "Be good for me. Don't make me punish you again today."

Her stomach clenched and her face heated, more so when she realized Sergio had heard.

Not trusting her voice to remain steady, she chose not to respond. Turning on her heel, which thankfully wasn't too high, she made her way down the hall away from him.

TOWER

ೞ ೞ ೞ

"Sergio says you gave him no trouble." Peter startled her with his sudden appearance, making her jolt. His hand rested on her shoulder, stilling her. "Sorry, didn't mean to scare you," he offered.

A gentle smile perched on his lips.

"I was watching…" She shrugged, unable to say what she'd been so enthralled with before he joined her.

She had no idea how long he'd been in his office working, but she'd managed to polish off three glasses of wine and too much of the crusty bread and cheese he'd had brought to her.

Peter glanced up at the main stage. A woman remained suspended in the intricate weavings of shibari bondage. Azalea knew the term because they had announced it when the couple began. Did Peter have the same skill as the man on stage?

"I thought you might like tonight's show." He took a seat beside her. A server placed a drink before him, and Peter thanked him before waving him off. Everything sort of appeared for him when he wanted it.

"I—" She shook her head, deciding not to ruin the casual ambiance with any more snark. "Yes. It's been entertaining. This is the second time he's tied her up. The first was like a spiderweb with her cocooned in the middle. Amazing, and beautiful." Azalea took another sip of her white wine. "And it takes so much time, so much patience."

"It does, yes. On both the part of the Top and the bottom." He brushed her hair from her shoulder. "If they weren't doing this as a performance tonight, Jerry would have her bound tighter, her breasts more prominent, and he'd be taking a flogger to her. She loves it best when she's bound tight with no wiggle room."

Azalea turned to him. Though there was a slight tilt to his

lips, giving her the impression he enjoyed the topic, he wasn't teasing her.

"A flogger to her breasts?" she asked sincerely.

"Oh, yes. And binding them makes them a bit more sensitive. It's perfectly safe, Azalea," he assured her.

She didn't comment on that. Even after he proved what an ass he could be, and after all she knew about the Titon family, she didn't doubt what he said.

She focused her attention on the couple who were ending their performance. Jerry brought his playmate down from the suspension binds with as much care and gentleness as she had been put in them.

"I was thinking." He cleared his throat before taking a sip of his drink.

She bit back another dig at him and drank wine instead.

His grin expressed his knowledge that she was trying at civility. Maybe at some point he would return it and let her go home. Or at the very least, explain why he wouldn't.

"You haven't questioned me about a cell phone, or worried about your mother calling you. Why?" He finished his drink. The ice clunked against the crystal glass.

"I've never needed a cell phone." No harm in telling the truth about it; he already knew her mother had been overprotective. "I usually had Santos or one of his men with me if I left the house." Which was pretty rare. And it wasn't like she had any friends to call even when she managed to get out of the house without an escort.

Peter tapped his finger against his chin, seeming to consider what she said then smiled a bit wider. "And now? When she calls home looking for you? Santos isn't around, from what my men have found. He ran away."

"Of course, he did." Azalea wouldn't expect that coward to stick around to feel her mother's wrath when she returned home to find her daughter kidnapped right from beneath his nose.

"Any idea where he would have run to? A different home? A vacation spot?" Peter pressed her, pushing her glass of wine out of her reach. The warm buzz of the alcohol worked its way through her, but she didn't need him to tell her when she'd had enough.

"No. We weren't exactly friends." Santos despised having to babysit her as much as she hated having him around.

Peter continued with his questions. "And your mother? Will she come home when she calls and no one answers?"

She shook her head and stood, taking a few steps to the railing where she looked down at the floor below where couples moved to the erotic beat of the music. She could almost pick out which women in the crowd were there for work and which were playing out pleasurable fantasies.

His body pressed against her from behind, his aftershave enveloping her.

"Do you know how to dance?" he asked.

"I do." Her mother had brought instructors into the house once a week during her teen years to teach her the art of dance. She knew some ballet, but mostly she'd been taught to dance at social gatherings. It had been one of the small shimmering lights of hope that her mother would allow her to be a normal woman and enter into society when she was old enough.

Without a word, he linked her hand with his and led her down the stairs to the main level and onto the dance floor.

At his gesture, a new song sprang to life from the bandstand next to the main stage. The crowd moved aside, giving Peter the room he seemed to demand.

Turning to her, he released her hand and offered his arms. She stepped into his embrace, holding his left hand with her right at shoulder height, and felt his right splay across her shoulder blades.

Apparently, he'd taken a few lessons himself.

Peter flashed her a smile and guided her into the first step as the singer began.

Azalea forced herself to focus on the paces, enjoying the fact they weren't dancing to any ballroom melody that her mother had forced upon her. But Peter wouldn't be ignored. His fingers touching her bare back reminded her with every step that he controlled her. Not only the dance.

"You took lessons?" she asked when his stare became too much to bear in silence.

"My mother's fault," he said with a hint of sadness. "My father couldn't dance to save his life and it was something she enjoyed. I was the next best thing, so she taught me."

Azalea imagined a young Peter dancing in a living room, dancing on a mother's feet. "Do your parents live far away?"

His eyes clouded, and he looked over her shoulder, turning her with a slight dip before answering. "My mother passed away a long time ago, my father right before her." His lips tightened as he spoke; his entire body beneath her touch tensed.

He spun her again, reeling her out and bringing her back in, closer to his body as he moved her along the dance floor.

"You didn't answer me about your mother," he said when she spoke again. Apparently, the topic of his family was off-limits. "Will she come running home when she calls and no one is there to answer?"

She took note of his set jaw and the firmness of his hold as the music continued. Reminding herself she'd decided to play nice with him in order to get answers, if not freedom, she answered him. "She's at some meeting and won't be home for a few more weeks. She rarely calls me if she's away for business, so she probably doesn't know I'm not at home.

If she's been in contact with Santos and he didn't tell her, she most likely won't know until she arrives home."

Peter's eyebrows shot up. "She doesn't call you while she's away? What sort of business is she in that she can't call her daughter?" The accusation in his questions wasn't lost on Azalea, and she couldn't blame him. From what little he'd told her of his own mother, of course, it would seem odd to him.

"I don't know what her business is, actually. She's always told me it's complicated." Azalea looked away from him, not wanting to see the disapproval in his features anymore.

"So, she won't know you aren't home for a few more weeks." He turned them again and picked up the steps to match the tempo of the music.

"Maybe I can be home before she gets back." Azalea took a chance. Either he would continue speaking freely with her, or he'd become agitated that she brought up her freedom again. "Maybe we can spend the next few weeks together, and I can go home before she returns. She promised we'd start looking for my own apartment when she was done with this meeting." She could hear the hope spring into her own voice.

He didn't react to her proposition. The dance continued, and he held her close as they made their way around the floor. The crowd had thinned once Peter began their waltz.

"If you spend the next few weeks with me, behaving, doing as you're told, and giving over to me, when your mother returns home, I'll let her know where you are. When she comes for you, we will decide what will happen then."

The song ended and with the last note, Azalea stopped dancing.

"What do you mean, give over to you?"

"I mean give me everything. Power, control, your submission. Give me all of you and when your mother returns, we'll decide what to do."

"I still don't understand why you won't just let me go. I don't understand why you took me in the first place. Can you at least give me that?" She searched his features, looking for a small beam of light. Something for her to latch onto that he wasn't a monster.

"I can't, no. I can give you my word you will be safe. I will never harm you—even when I hurt you."

They stood while dancers filled the floor, surrounding them. The band struck up a fast-paced song.

"When she returns. You promise?"

"I swear it." He held her hands and gave them both a squeeze, his stare boring into hers.

She swept her gaze over the alcoves overlooking the dance floor. The moving artwork of submission and dominance. Another couple was taking the main stage followed by two uniformed staff members rolling a spanking bench into place.

Everything she'd come to this club to see, to feel, to learn about, he was offering to her. And in the end, she could have complete freedom. From him, from her mother. She'd figure out the hows later.

"Okay. I agree." She pulled free of his grip and thrust her hand out to him. A business agreement began with a handshake. She knew that much.

He looked at her offering and chuckled, taking it between both of his.

"Let's get home, then." He turned her and escorted her toward the exit.

"What's on the upper floors of this building?" she asked once they were in the back hall headed toward the garage. Staircases went upward into darkness, and she'd seen an elevator.

"The girls who get work privileges here are also able to rent the rooms on three of the floors to do business. We provide security for them, so it's safer for them to stay here than to go to a motel down the street or out to some asshole's car." Peter grabbed her coat from one of his men and helped her into it.

"The three floors above those are going to be mine once construction is complete. I didn't want to hold off on the club while my private rooms were being finished," he continued to explain as he took her to the garage where he'd parked his car.

Azalea thanked the man holding her door open as she climbed into the passenger seat.

She had more questions for him, but when he took his spot behind the wheel and turned the music on, she figured he didn't want to play twenty questions.

And she didn't want to jeopardize the gift he was giving her. Hope. In a few weeks, she would be free.

CHAPTER 10

*P*eter escorted Azalea up the steps to the house with his hand on her back, wishing her coat wasn't barring him from feeling her skin. He hadn't taken much time to pick a dress for her; he'd simply grabbed a black dress from Ellie's closet, positive she'd forgive him the intrusion.

But to see it on Azalea, the way it flowed over her gentle curves, highlighted her generous breasts, and showcased the muscles in her back when she moved—Ellie would have to buy herself a new dress when she got home.

The front door opened as they approached. Daniel stood with his hand out, gripping a cell phone, and a quick glance at Azalea on Peter's arm.

"What's wrong?" Peter asked, stepping through the door and helping Azalea with her coat. She remained silent, taking in the foyer, and he realized she hadn't been given a proper tour of the house. The way her eyes widened at the artwork and architecture of the narrow area made him want to show her Ellie's art gallery. His cousin's wife had a gift with the paintbrush.

"Aubree," Daniel said, shoving his phone into his back pocket. "I was just heading out. She went to Sampson's tonight, looking for a shift. When Sarah reminded her she was off duty for the time being, she threw a fucking fit."

Peter sighed. He'd forgotten all about Aubree. When was the last time he'd forgotten about delivering a punishment to one of the girls? Had it ever happened?

"I should have dealt with her by now." Peter glanced at Azalea. She seemed focused on a painting, but he knew her better. She was listening to every word.

"I told Sarah to keep her there, give her something to do, and I'd pick her up," Daniel explained.

"Okay. I'll talk with her first thing tomorrow. Tell her to meet me at eight."

"Got it." He glanced at Azalea. "You sure you don't want me to take care of it?"

Peter would like nothing more than to hand off his responsibilities, but until Ash made it back home, he was keeping things as they were.

"No. I got it. Get her back here and remind her that if she would prefer to leave our employment, she's more than free to do so."

Daniel started to speak, but shook his head and clammed up. With a curt nod, he stalked through the door, pulling it shut behind him.

Azalea folded her arms over her stomach, taking another step toward the stairs.

Peter pulled one hand free and linked it with his, walking her up to his room. She'd agreed to give him everything, and he wouldn't wait any longer to claim what was his.

"What did you mean when you said you should have dealt with her?" Azalea asked once inside his bedroom. She walked to the far corner of the room, away from the door leading to his private playroom, and away from him.

"Exactly what you think it means," he answered, shaking his suit jacket off and tossing it on an armchair.

"How you dealt with me this morning?" she asked. Her fingers were twirling her long hair, but he didn't see any actual fear in her eyes. She might be nervous—and she should be—but she wasn't afraid of him.

"Well, not as severe. She won't be as stubborn as you." He smiled.

"She'll just—I mean you'll—" The deep blush that took over her face couldn't have been more beautiful.

Peter held back his laugh, not wanting her to misunderstand and think he was laughing at her. That didn't mean he didn't intend on using her embarrassment to push her a little further.

"I'll make her bend over the spanking bench we have in one of the offices in the Annex and bare her ass for me. Then we'll discuss what she did wrong, and as long as she doesn't give me any attitude, I'll give her ten lashes with a belt."

She hadn't blinked while he spoke. She didn't make a sound or protest when he made his way over to her.

"What did she do wrong?" Azalea asked, finally breaking her silence.

Peter tilted his head. "Well, I wouldn't tell her how you've been naughty, so I can't tell you how she was naughty, either."

She nodded, and just like that she seemed to snap out of her trance.

"She's agreed to this? I mean, she's your employee, right? Isn't that like—assault?"

Peter chuckled. "No, it's not assault, and she's fully consented to the consequences for breaking the house rules."

He placed his hands on her slender shoulders. Sliding his hands behind her, he unzipped the dress. "But we aren't talking about her anymore. Right now, I want you to take this dress off and let me see you."

"I don't think—"

"You did agree, remember? At the club?" He let her go and backed off. He wouldn't force her, and he wouldn't disrobe her. She would do this, and she would do it on her own.

"Well, yes, but I didn't think—"

"You thought we'd come home and snuggle up in front of the TV?" He couldn't remember the last time he'd watched television.

"Take off the dress, Azalea," he ordered when she didn't respond or start moving. "I've already seen you naked." Except this time, he'd be paying a hell of a lot more attention to what was standing before him.

He didn't take his gaze off her. It would make it easier for her if he wasn't looking, but that wasn't the point.

She brushed the thin straps from her shoulders and let the dress slide down her body and pool at her feet. He kept his eyes focused on hers, enjoying the blush creeping down her neck and across her chest.

"Your hair. Put it behind you." He wiggled his fingers at her.

She started to roll her eyes, but stopped. He'd let it go this time; she did catch herself after all. And he wasn't a complete asshole.

Well, not at the moment, anyway.

She swiped her hair behind her shoulders, leaving her breasts completely exposed. Her nipples beaded up nicely with the slight chill in the room. Perfectly round, pert pink nipples.

He stopped himself from licking his lips. No need to frighten her even more than she probably already was.

"Other than me, has any other man seen you naked?" he asked, making his way back to her.

She shook her head, bowing it.

"No. Look up." He would not allow her to hide within herself, or to cower from him. The woman with the determination and steel in her spine, that's who he wanted in his bed. He may bend her to his will, and he would dominate her every move, but he did not want a wallflower in his fucking bed.

When her eyes met his again, he half expected to see tears shining there, but saw none. The blush had even faded.

"Now, answer me with your mouth," he said, lifting her chin with his fingertips. "While I still allow you to have use of it."

The blush returned. Beautiful. She knew exactly what he meant. Or, at least, she thought she did. So many ways to take away her use of her mouth. A gag. His cock. The thought of putting his dick between her lips made him shudder.

"No. No one but you," she answered, and it took a moment for him to register what she was talking about. He needed to stop fantasizing and start doing.

"Does that mean you haven't been touched, either?"

"I've never had sex before if that's what you mean." She rolled her shoulders back. A pretense of bravado if he ever saw one. She may want him to think she was proud of holding onto her virginity for so long, but he knew better. She'd been held back by her mother in every way.

"Hmmm." He dropped his hand from her chin and lightly traced the muscle of her neck down to her collarbone, noticing the sweet shudder run through her. "But you've touched yourself. You've had an orgasm before." He didn't ask; he simply stated what he thought to be fact.

"Does that matter?"

He chuckled, slipping his hand farther down into the valley between her breasts.

"No, but I want to know. Have you played with your tits before?" He went for crude. "And remember, you agreed to give me your full submission. If you lie, I'll know, and you'll be ass up over my lap instead flat on your back."

Her tongue ran across her bottom lip. Was she unsure how to answer? Could she possibly be ashamed at having touched her beautiful breasts?

"Yes, I have." She breathed out the words as though it took a weight off her. "Of course, I have."

He waved at the bed. "Lie back on the bed and show me."

"I—"

Stilling her with a finger over her lips, he shook his head. "No more arguing or overthinking. Right now, you're going to do exactly what you're told to do without hesitation, or I'll go in my playroom and get some of my less pleasant toys."

She gave a gentle nod, and he helped her climb onto the bed, enjoying the strain and pull of her leg and ass muscles as she moved. Fuck, she was gorgeous.

"On your back. Move up on the pillows. There's a good girl," he said. Sitting on the bed beside her, he pulled her leg toward him then lifted it and moved to sit inside her spread limbs.

Her face reddened so easily, so purely, it took his breath away.

"Show me." He rested his hand on the inside of her thigh, feeling the warmth of her skin.

He took a moment to enjoy his fill of her. The softness of her curves, the gentle flutter of her stomach as she tried to control her breathing. She may be panicked, but she wasn't trying to get away or take back her promise.

Running his hand from her knee down her thigh to her sex, he grinned at finding no patch of curls.

"You're bare," he said more to himself than her, and touched the spot where many women had silky hair. She sucked in her breath when he moved lower, stroking her lips. Wet. As they should be. His inspection aroused her.

"I—" She tried to close her legs, but a harsh slap to her inner thigh stilled her. "Ow!"

"It will be much worse if you disobey again. Keep your legs spread. I want to see your cunt," he chastised in a firm voice.

Her eyes widened, and she made fists at her sides, but she didn't speak. Good girl. He didn't want to spend the evening disciplining her. As much as he enjoyed the act, he wanted to fondle and lick every inch of her. Show her there was much pleasure to be had in obedience.

Using his thumb and his forefinger, he pried open her lips, finding the pink, wet flesh of her pussy. Her swollen clit begged for a kiss, but he had already given her directions. It was time for her to show him she would behave as promised.

"Go on, Azalea. Show me how you play with yourself. Show me how you pet your pussy when no one's around to see or hear."

She averted her stare, creeping her hands from her sides to between her delicious thighs. He watched her, thinking to give her some solace in that he wasn't staring directly at her face. Let her hide a bit, for now, but soon she wouldn't be able to hide from either of them.

Keeping her lips spread, he watched her fingers slip between his hands and find the nub. A soft moan escaped her the moment the pad of her finger brushed the sensitive bundle of nerves.

"That's it, good girl, play with your clit," he whispered, as though she were an animal in the wild he didn't want to disturb.

She pressed her middle finger down on the swollen bud and moved in circles. He chanced a quick glance up at her and found her eyes closed. Perfect.

"Nice." He released her lips and sprawled out on his stomach, with her pussy mere inches away from his face. "Keep going," he ordered, when she paused. His movements had drawn her out of whatever aroused fantasy she'd slipped into.

He could make her keep her eyes on him. He shouldn't let her dive into her mind in order to escape him, but she had such an innocence about her, corrupting her too soon might break her. And he didn't break his toys.

Her finger disappeared from her clit, and he followed her movements as she stuck it into her mouth, sucking on it briefly. His cock ached beneath him when her wet digit went back to rolling the hard clit around and around.

"Fuck." He breathed out, blowing his breath onto her exposed sex.

She moaned and rubbed herself with all of her fingers. Round and around she went. Her hips came off the bed slightly but enough for him to see the juices starting to coat her sex. The girl was soaked.

Tired of being the standby, he grabbed her. Her eyes flew open, and he kept her locked in his gaze. Not saying a word, he took her hand and brought it to his mouth. He ran his tongue over her fingertips, taking off every bit of her arousal and groaning over the sweetness of it.

"My turn," he said with a gruffness and put her hand on her belly. "Now, you keep your hands out of my way."

He lowered himself to her sex, inhaling the aroma before flicking his tongue lightly over her clit.

Her sharp inhale of breath drove him closer to the brink. A man could hold himself back for so long before erupting into action. Scooting down a fraction, he slid both arms beneath her ass and brought her off the bed, feeding himself with her pussy.

"Oh. Oh," she moaned when his tongue darted into her

entrance. So much heat, so much delectable flavor. He ran his tongue up her slit, suckling on her clit before sinking his teeth into her.

"Oh fuck," she breathed. He didn't look up at her, but he could feel her moving. She was half sitting, half lying down to watch him.

Let her. The watching made it easier for her to lose herself in what he was doing to her. What he would be doing to her, what he'd been waiting to do since he'd laid eyes on her at Tower.

"Peter." She lifted her hips toward him. Whether she did it on purpose or not didn't matter. His girl was seeking her release.

He pulled back from her, looking up the length of her body at her aroused expression. Bottom lip tucked between her teeth, hair framing her perfectly blushed face.

"What do you want, Azalea?" he asked, rubbing his chin over her clit, knowing any touch at this point dragged her to the edge.

War raged in her expression. She wanted to ask for her release, wanted to scream at him to make her come. He knew it. But then there was the sensible, stubborn Azalea fighting it.

"I'll make you come. All you have to do is ask." He nuzzled her sensitive bits again, enjoying the way her eyelids fluttered and her breath huffed from between her swollen lips. Someone had been biting down hard to keep from crying out.

"Don't make me," she pleaded so softly, so prettily his cock twitched. She didn't understand how much her distress turned him on.

"You don't have to. If you don't ask, you won't come. But I'll keep you in this state, this high of arousal on the peak of explosion for a very, very long time. You'll wish you'd asked."

As always, he meant what he said. If she didn't ask, he'd edge her to the brink of insanity. She'd be begging for release, but the time would have passed when he would grant her request, and the poor girl would go to bed so aroused she probably wouldn't sleep at all.

While staring at her, he slipped one hand from beneath her ass and gingerly glided a finger into her pussy entrance.

"Oh!" She gripped the bedsheets and tried to wiggle away, but he whipped his free hand out and pressed down on her belly, keeping her exactly where he wanted her.

"None of that. Be a good girl and take my finger. Just one, I promise." He pushed his middle finger all the way into her passage, feeling the heat and squeeze of her channel. "See, no pain. Only pleasure." He kissed her lips then moved back to her clit.

"Peter. Oh god. Peter. Okay, okay." He kept his gaze up at her while he suckled her clit again. She threw her head back and leaned against her elbows. "Please. Please, make me."

He gave her a final lick then released her. "Make you what?"

Did she just growl? He grinned up at the fiery woman glaring down at him.

"Please make me—argh—" She fought herself much harder than him. "Please make me come." Her face flamed red with the words, but he could see the arousal in her body ramp up at being made to say them. Her nipples tightened, her tummy tensed, and her pussy gripped his finger even tighter.

"Do you want to come hard?" he asked, no sense in wasting the opportunity.

Her eyes widened at his question.

"Do you want me to make you come hard, or soft. Like one of those little orgasms that leave you unsatisfied. You'll need to specify." He was being an ass, but he didn't much care.

When she didn't respond he curled his finger inside her and stroked the inner walls until he found her sweet spot.

"Hard. Make me come hard. Please!" she begged. Oh, how pretty she was when she pleaded him.

He continued to stroke her while thrusting in and out of her.

"Imagine this being my cock. Me fucking you so hard you can't remember to breathe. That's going to happen, Azalea. I promise you that." He wouldn't be able to wait very long, but he wouldn't fuck her tonight. Not when he had her so pliable and accepting. No, tonight he'd teach her obedience was rewarded in the most pleasurable of ways.

He licked her pussy again, up her length and down while he finger fucked her, nipping at her clit but not giving it his full attention. Not yet, not until the walls of her pussy trembled.

"Please. Please, Peter. Please make me come," she chanted in a heavy whisper. He doubted she even recognized it was herself saying the words.

Her body tensed, and he moved his ministrations to her clit, sucking it between his teeth, biting down and flicking his tongue over it all at the same time.

She exploded.

The scream she released was completely intelligible, and her hips bucked up at him while he continued to fuck her harder and faster with his finger, driving her through the waves of her orgasm.

Slowing his movements, he brought her back down from her high. Removing his finger, he licked it clean then placed a gentle kiss on her sex.

Her chest rose and fell hard as she gasped for air, her face more flushed than before. She'd come hard for him. Such a good girl.

"No, don't move." He laid a flat hand on her thighs when she moved.

"We aren't done yet."

CHAPTER 11

Azalea tried to catch her breath and focus her mind at the same time. It wasn't working. Peter looked tense. Not quite angry, but not his relaxed self.

She realized she was still spread out for him, completely naked and completely vulnerable. Her first reaction was to snap her legs closed, but he knelt between them, making it impossible. He wasn't exactly the easiest man to move.

"Have you ever watched a dirty movie?" he asked, reaching out to her.

"Like porn? No." She shook her head.

He chuckled. "Of all the things to lie about, you choose that?"

Her damn cheeks heated again. How could a man make her blush so fucking easily? It was though he held some remote to her emotions and could flick them on or off at will.

Of course, she'd seen porn movies. Her mother blocked some but not all of her Internet access. Finding spanking and kinky videos hadn't been hard, and she'd been surprised she'd been able to access them.

"We'll discuss honesty in the morning. For now, I want you to answer truthfully."

Fine. Asshole.

"I've seen a few videos." Okay, not totally true, but it was all she would give him.

"It's going to be a long discussion, I see." If he hadn't smiled when he said it, her heart might have been able to slow down. But when he flashed that grin of his, the one where that damn dimple showed up, she couldn't help but weaken a bit for him.

"So, you've seen a man's cock, at least on screen?"

"Yes," she answered, letting him pull her up to a full sitting position.

"Good. Get on the floor, on your knees for me, Azalea," he instructed and moved out of the way, giving her space to swing her legs to the side and slide out of bed.

She moved down to her knees, feeling the lush carpeting beneath her, and looked up at him. Any fear she expected to experience at kneeling before him evaporated when he stood in front of her, hands on his belt.

"Palms on your thighs, spread your legs. I want to see your pussy whenever you're on your knees like this for me. You don't hide anything from me, Azalea. Nothing." He stroked her hair, soothing both the flyaway strands and her worry.

A part of her told her to rebel. To fight against this man who'd stolen her away, but she'd agreed. She'd said she'd be his until her mother returned. She couldn't back down now just because she was unsure of what was coming next and uncomfortable with her inexperience.

"Stop overthinking," he said, running his hand down her head and picking up a long lock of hair. She watched as he dragged his finger along the length of it.

She sat back on her heels, spread her thighs, and rested

her palms on her knees. Not sure where to put her stare, she focused on the floor, fixated on his feet. He still wore his dress shoes.

Azalea realized he hadn't undressed at all except for removing his suit jacket. There she knelt before him, nude, post orgasm, and he stood completely guarded against her.

"See, I can touch and kiss and punish almost every part of you." He let go of her hair and leaned farther down to tweak her nipple. "No." He slapped her breast when she jerked back from his touch. "You never pull away from me, Azalea. You've given yourself to me—temporarily, I know—and you'll follow every order, every rule, or you'll be very sorry."

Against what she knew was right, her body ached for him more with his dictate. The sternness in his voice shouldn't have acted as such an aphrodisiac, but now that the threat of never seeing her mother again was gone, she was able to melt into his dominance.

She nodded, not trusting her voice not to betray her.

He went back to work on his buckle, and she watched as he let the leather hang from his hips. The button on his pants and the zipper came next, and she found herself licking her lips with anticipation.

She'd seen a man's dick on a screen, but never in person.

He shoved his pants and boxers down his hips until his cock sprang free. She swallowed hard and intently stared at his member bobbing in front of her. His hand gripped the long, thick shaft at the base and stroked upward to the tip of his head where a small bead of pre-cum formed.

Without thinking, she stuck out her tongue and leaned forward, taking the pearl onto her tongue and swallowed it. Salty. Manly.

Delicious.

Peter chuckled. "Did I say you could lick my cock yet?" he asked.

Her eyes flew open and met his. Although he'd laughed, there was little merriment in his tone.

"You weren't honest with me a few minutes ago. You let lies come out of that pretty mouth of yours." He reminded her of the tiny white lie she'd told. But he'd said they would discuss it in the morning. It wasn't morning.

Before she could voice her objection to his decree, he laid two fingers over her lips and shook his head.

"Nope. You lost the privilege to use your mouth."

What the hell did that mean?

She didn't have much time to think on it, as he yanked his belt free from his pants and shoved the leather into her mouth. Pulling it behind her head, he shoved the belt through the buckle and tightened it until her lips were spread wide with the strap between her teeth and her head being controlled by him.

"Cup your hands together," he ordered, his tone back to being harsh and unyielding.

She positioned herself like he directed, and he pulled them up until they were as high as her lips.

He switched his hold on the belt to his left hand, and wrapped the right around his cock again. She wanted to taste him again, to lick the silky skin under the head. She craved to take him in her mouth as she'd seen all those women do in the movies. But he'd taken away her mouth. The leather stretched her skin, biting into the corners of her lips.

"Keep those beautiful blue eyes on my cock. Watch what you can't have. If you'd been honest, you'd have your lips around me instead of watching me jerk off." His voice tightened as he stroked himself.

A bit of saliva ran down her chin. She wanted to swipe it away, but he yanked on the belt keeping her steady. Was there anything he didn't see when he looked at her? It was as though he could read her thoughts before they even fully formed in her mind.

He cupped his hand below her chin, gathering her spit. "There. That's going to be much better." He smeared her saliva along his shaft and went back to stroking his cock.

"Fuck, that's good," he said, taking a tiny step toward her. His scent wafted to her nostrils; more drool fell from her chin, landing on her naked breasts.

"Such a messy girl," he chastised but didn't slow his movements. "No. Don't look away. You watch. You watch what you can't have because you lied."

She snapped her attention back to his actions, willing her body to stop reacting. She'd just had a mind-blowing orgasm; how could she be so wanton and eager to have his tongue and fingers on her again? She'd been horny before, but never had she felt so damn empty as she did watching him pump his thick cock through his own fist.

She wanted it. She wanted his taste, his feel, she wanted to devour him, and she wanted him inside of her.

It hadn't been a big lie. A tiny fabrication of the truth to protect her pride. Why did he have to retaliate with such cruelty?

She'd rather have a spanking. Couldn't he just spank her a little instead?

"Oh fuck." He came forward again, his cock almost touching her fingertips.

The belt pulled tighter.

"Fuck."

She moved her gaze up to his face, and found him staring down at her. His face flushed, his nostrils flared, and his hair hanging down around his eyes.

"Catch it all, Azalea," he ground out, jerking her head downward and making her watch him again.

Long, hot spurts of cum shot out of his cock, landing in

her palms. He continued to jerk himself, aiming toward her outreached hands. He grunted and pulled the belt tighter, amping the discomfort in her lips up another notch.

But nothing compared to the longing she felt at watching the strings of his cum land on her palms, across her fingers, but none coming close to her mouth.

When he finished, he stroked his clock slow, bringing the last drop of his seed to the tip and wiping it on her fingers.

"Hold that," he ordered, letting go of the belt and leaning back against the bead catching his breath. The belt loosened, and she could have spit out the leather if she'd dared.

But she didn't.

She moved her hands to form a deeper cup and held his load between them. Making sure to not let a drop leak out. It was warm, sticky, and she could smell his fragrance.

The desire to lick herself clean overwhelmed her and, for a moment, she wondered if the punishment for her presumptuous behavior would be worth the joy of feeling his cum on her tongue.

"Put your hands together." He stood and yanked his pants back up, buttoning them.

Her heart sank, but she pressed her palms together.

Peter tightened the belt again and pulled upward. "On your feet, Azalea."

She managed to stand, still holding her hands in a prayer position. He led her by the belt to the attached washroom where he took the gag out of her mouth and dropped the belt onto the counter. She worked her lips open and closed, getting the sting out of them.

He watched her silently, as though deciding what to do with her next. His cum had cooled in her hands, and the idea of licking them clean no longer aroused her like it had in the thrilling moment of his orgasm.

"Wash up." He turned the water on in the sink and stood

by with his arms folded over his chest, watching her as she rinsed off his cum. "Next time, you'll lick your hands clean, but not until my cum has dried on your skin."

She nodded, and reached for a towel.

He took the towel from her and patted her hands until they were dry. She looked up at him, feeling a sense of shame. She'd let him suckle her pussy, she'd come hard, so fucking hard and loud—screaming like a wanton woman in his room, and then she'd let him come on her. And she'd loved it. All of it. Every second, even when he denied her. When he'd punished her for such a small dishonesty. She'd loved it.

"You're overthinking again." He smiled gently at her, pushing her hair behind her again. "So much hair."

"My mother told me my sister kept hers short. I grew mine out so—" She stilled her tongue and swallowed back the words. She'd never said them before.

"So, your mother would maybe see you as different. So, she'd know you weren't your sister." Peter filled in the blanks all on his own. He didn't need her to spell anything out for him; he seemed to know everything.

"Yeah," she whispered.

He turned her to face the mirror while he moved behind her. Pulling all of her hair into one thick ponytail, he separated the bundle and began braiding it. She watched him in the mirror, the intense concentration displayed on his features.

Although he was focused, he didn't have the tense look she'd grown accustomed to seeing. He seemed more relaxed, more at peace.

When he reached the end, he held onto it with one hand and reached around her, opening drawers until he found a rubber band. She didn't tell him that it was going to hurt like hell to take the band off in the morning. Disturbing him would change the atmosphere, and for the first time since she arrived, she felt the tension leaving her body.

"Let's get you to bed." He linked his fingers through hers and tugged her along.

Once she was beneath the covers, he leaned over her, staring into her eyes.

"I have a few things to see to and then I'll be up. I want you to sleep, Azalea. No snooping around or leaving the bedroom, okay?"

"I'll stay here," she promised with a yawn.

He ran a finger across her brow. "You look so sweet after an orgasm. Maybe I should keep you in this state all the time."

His lips pressed against hers, firmly.

"Good night, Peter," she mumbled when he stood back to full height. Rolling over to her side, her back facing him, she squeezed her eyes shut and brought her knees up to her chest.

Another ache formed. Not quite loneliness. She had grown adept at fighting that away over the years, but of hope. Hope that when it was all over, when her mother returned and he allowed her freedom, that she would be able to piece together a life that included everything he'd given her and more.

Whatever that was.

CHAPTER 12

Peter walked into the Annex, his belly full of eggs and sausage, and his mind fully fixated on the beautiful blond he'd shared his breakfast with.

He hadn't expected her to wake up so early, but when he'd come out of the shower, she was sitting in the bed with the covers pulled up to her chin.

After a short discussion on why she needed actual clothes to walk around in, he produced a pair of jeans and a sweater. He'd had Tommy go shopping with one of the girls from the Annex to pick out some items for Azalea. And it had been successful. She had thanked him for the clothes and jumped right into them.

He had helped her unbraid her long hair but let her handle the brushing of it. He'd simply leaned against the doorjamb and watched her.

But, now, he had to get to work. Dealing with Aubree couldn't be put off any longer. He hadn't brought it up during breakfast, and Azalea seemed to have forgotten. Not that anything she said would have changed his course of action, but he didn't want to argue with her and have to punish her as well.

He hadn't intended to punish her at all the previous night, but that little white lie had popped out of her mouth so freely, he couldn't let it slide. Jerking off into her hands instead of plowing into that beautiful mouth of hers had been punishment for him as much as her. He had seen the desire in her eyes. She had wanted to suck him, and lick him, and he'd used the image of her doing so along with his thick belt tied around her mouth to find his release quickly.

He still needed to talk with her about honesty, but it wasn't the punishment she probably thought was coming. Discipline and punishment weren't always the same thing. She needed to learn the rules, and he found most submissive women learned them best bent over with a paddle in his hand.

Adjusting his hard cock in his slacks, he stopped outside the door to his office. He had been told Aubree was inside waiting for him, and he'd let her stew long enough. Hell, he probably owed her an apology for not completing the punishment in a timely fashion. He had, after all, caused her to lose an extra shift.

"Peter." Tommy joined him at the door. "Azalea is looking for you."

Peter looked past him, down the hall leading to the main house.

"I just left her. She's supposed to be in Ash's office." He'd given her the code to his laptop so she could get online. She didn't have any social media accounts from what his men had found, but she did play around with graphic design.

"Well, she's not. She's at the door." Tommy jerked a thumb at the door separating the Annex from the main house.

He clenched his teeth and took a deep breath. Aubree shouldn't have to keep waiting.

"Tell her I'll be with her in an hour and to go back to the office like I told her," he said grabbing the door handle to the office.

"I did tell her that," Tommy argued. "She's insisting."

Peter narrowed his gaze. "Are you telling me you can't get that slip of a woman to go back to the damn office?" She was beautiful, but she wasn't a goddamn witch. What sort of spell did that woman cast over his men?

"Are you telling me I can use the same force I would with any of the other girls who didn't listen?" Tommy rolled his shoulders back, straightening his spine. He had a point. If Peter wouldn't let him use the authority he had, why the hell would Azalea listen to him?

Peter exhaled. "Fuck no." No one was touching her but him. "Stay here," he ordered, and marched off to deal with Azalea.

He flung the door open and found her wringing her hands. "Do you ever stay where you are put? You were supposed to wait in the office," he said.

She moved up to her toes, trying to look past him down the hall.

"You didn't do it already, did you?" she asked.

"Do what? Stop fidgeting." He placed his hand over hers and drew her attention to him.

"Punish that girl?"

A soft blush blossomed on her cheeks, and even though she'd calmed her movements, she continued to try and see past him.

Was she jealous?

"No. I was about to speak with her," he said.

"You said you'd give me a tour of the estate." She looked at him. Like she'd just found a way to keep him from going through with it.

Making Aubree wait any longer would be cruel. Though

he would rather be giving Azalea the tour he had promised her.

"You said you'd stay in the office. I told you I'd come for you when I was finished. Now go back to the office," he said, not missing that he sounded more like a father figure than the man who possessed her every fiber. The woman was twisting him from the inside, making him coddle when he should be disciplining.

She didn't respond. Moving back up to her toes, she looked around him, trying to see past him into the Annex. He knew she had a curiosity about her, and he couldn't blame her, given the way she seemed to have been raised, but he'd already given his order. He'd told her to wait for him. He'd told her to go back, and still she defied him.

"Okay, have it your way." He grabbed hold of her elbow and led her into the Annex, not bothering to lock the door behind him as she was the person in the house he'd been trying to keep out.

Tommy had a mixture of pleasure and uncertainty in his expression when he noticed his boss dragging Azalea toward the room.

"Don't fucking stand there. Open the damn door," Peter lashed out at him. Tommy jolted into motion, pulling the door open for him.

Azalea tried to pull away.

"Peter! No. I don't want to watch!" She tried to push his hand off her arm.

Once in the room, Peter, completely ignoring Aubree standing in the center, spun Azalea to face him. The door had shut behind him, and Tommy stood on the other side. If she decided to bolt, he'd catch her in no time at all.

"You aren't here to watch," he declared. She could think whatever she wanted to about that. He had a damn job to do, and he was going to do it and get it over with.

"Now." He took a deep breath and turned to Aubree. "I seem to have two girls who don't know how to follow rules or directions. So." He took a few steps away from Azalea, needing space so as not to touch her. He felt the fear start to rise in her and, with it, a temptation to soothe her.

"So. In the interest of time, I'll be dealing with you both at the same time."

Aubree held any objection she may have had. It wasn't the first time she'd been in this room with another woman. There was no intimacy between Peter and any of the girls of the Annex. Although he did prefer to deal with them one on one when they earned a house punishment, he didn't feel it was always necessary or to be expected.

"You can't," Azalea said, eyes wide and hands wringing again.

"I don't think now would be a good time to tell me what I can and can't do," he shot at her. "Aubree. Are you free to come and go as you wish?"

"Yes, sir," she answered softly, submissively with her eyes cast down at the floor. Maybe Azalea would learn a thing or two during the session.

"The only stipulation is what?" he asked, folding his arms over his chest. Azalea still fidgeted off to the side, but he kept his focus on Aubree.

"We need to sign in and out so the house knows where we are."

"And why do we do this?" He'd gone through this script so many damn times, he felt more like a damn recording than a disciplinarian.

"For our safety, sir." Aubree's response came as automatically as his questions.

"Where did you go that night?" he asked.

She glanced up at him but lowered her gaze when he raised his eyebrows.

"I went out with some friends. To a bar on the north side," her answer came softly. He didn't usually probe into the social activity of the girls. They weren't slaves, after all, and were entitled to their privacy.

"Did you have a good time?" he asked. From the corner of his vision, he could make out Azalea staring at Aubree.

"Yes, sir."

"Good. You aren't going to have a good time right now, though, are you?" he asked moving toward the large leather couch pushed up against the far wall of the office.

"No, sir." She kept her eyes down, but Azalea freely watched him move about the office. So much for her taking a cue from Aubree.

"Please explain to Azalea what happens when the rules are disobeyed." He pointed at Azalea, whose face had reddened nicely since he started talking.

"Uh." Aubree sounded hesitant. He had strayed from the usual script of these discipline sessions.

"Go on," Peter prompted as he pushed the couch away from the wall and several feet toward the middle of the room.

"When we break a rule, we are given a spanking or are taken off duty." She paused. "Which means we can't earn any money."

"They ground you from income?" Azalea asked with a hushed whisper.

Aubree let out a soft giggle. "I suppose so. It's not usually very long, but this time—" she stopped talking and looked over at Peter. He caught her short glare but didn't rebuke her for it. She wasn't wrong.

"Azalea, tell Aubree what happens to naughty little submissive girls who don't stay where they're put." Happy with his placement of the couch, he put his hands on his hips and watched Azalea's eyes widen and her mouth drop open.

Aubree wouldn't get much out of the session other than paying her consequence and getting back on the roster for work at the clubs or taking clients at the Annex. But Azalea had some learning to do.

"Now, Azalea," he said with a firmer tone when she seemed to have shut down.

"I suppose you spank them, too." She thrust that damn chin of hers out again.

Peter couldn't help but grin, and he noticed the slight upturn of Aubree's lips as well.

"You suppose correctly," he deadpanned. "Both of you here and bend over the back of the couch." He patted the leather padding.

Aubree didn't argue, simply walked over and did as instructed. She wasn't a short woman by any means, so she could still keep her feet flat on the floor while draped over the back. She'd worn a skirt for her meeting with him, which he appreciated. Made his job a bit easier.

"Azalea. Now. Or we can discuss this again upstairs when we are finished here." As it was, she'd already taken away the playful spanking he'd wanted to give her after he was finished with Aubree. He wouldn't play with her after he punished her, at least not until a few hours passed. No sense in mixing business with pleasure and ruining all the work the punishment had done.

As though her feet were lodged in cement blocks, Azalea trudged to the couch. She gave him another glare when she pressed her legs against the leather but didn't try to talk him out of it. With as much grace as she could, she climbed into position beside Aubree. Being much shorter than Aubree, she had to stand on tiptoe. But her ass wasn't as high as he wanted it, so he'd have to fix that.

First, he went to Aubree and flipped her skirt up her back. No panties. Good girl. Then he moved over to Azalea, reached in front of her to undo her jeans, and tugged them down. She grunted when he pulled them to her knees and a hand flew back when her ass was completely exposed.

"None of that." He smacked her hand and pushed it away from his target. Gripping her hips, he manhandled her until her ass was the same height as Aubree's, making her feet dangle in the air.

He could imagine the fury in her eyes at being put in such a position, but she had no one to blame but herself.

Peter worked the buckle open and ripped the leather from his pants. Two sets of naked buttocks clenched at the sound.

He really did have a good job.

Folding over the leather, he stepped up to Aubree first. Let Azalea hear the spanking and wait for her own. Maybe the anticipation would get her head in the right spot.

"Ten, and I don't want to hear a sound, Aubree." He placed his hand flat on the small of her back to keep her steady and delivered the standard punishment. Other than a gasp and groan, she remained quiet during the spanking.

Peter watched her ass bounce beneath his belt as the creamy skin morphed into a rosy blush. But what kept drawing his attention was Azalea peeking over her shoulder to see the punishment being given.

"Eyes forward, Azalea," he finally ordered when his cock reacted to her brazen snooping. It wasn't unusual for his dick to get hard during a punishment. He wouldn't act on it, but he wouldn't deny watching beautiful asses burn up beneath his punishing hand got him hard.

This time was different. It wasn't until his eyes met Azalea's that he felt anything other than duty.

He finished the last stroke of Aubree's punishment.

"Think you can remember to sign out next time you go out?" he asked the back of her head.

"Yes, sir." She nodded. He doubted it would be the last time she'd break the rule. Whether she actually forgot or because she just wanted a taste of true discipline, she'd find herself in this exact position soon enough.

He flipped her skirt down and helped her to stand from the couch.

"You shouldn't have had to wait so long for this discussion, so you'll be paid for the last two shifts you missed." He patted her hands and let them go.

"What about the tips I missed?" she asked, her fingers fidgeting at her sides. Experienced or not, her ass was probably on fire and, as soon as she was out of his sight, she'd be rubbing it out.

"Don't push it," he said with a cocked brow. "Go stand in front of Azalea. Hold her hands for her. She won't be able to stop from reaching back, and I don't want to hurt her," he instructed, noting the tension creep into Azalea's body at his words.

"Yes, sir." She dropped her gaze and went around the couch. Kneeling on the cushions, she reached out for Azalea. "It's okay, hon," Peter heard her whisper. "Ten isn't so bad."

Hmm. Maybe it was time to increase the strokes for the more experienced submissives in their employ.

"Give her your hands, Azalea. You wanted so badly to be here, now you're here." He touched her ass with his fingers. He never touched the Annex girls in such a way during their punishments. No intimacy, but Azalea wasn't one of the Annex girls.

Peter saw Aubree catch the touch, and a soft frown appear on her lips. Maybe it was time he spoke with her about putting herself up for a long-term contract. Maybe she was ready for more than short-term clients and hour sessions.

Once Azalea's hands were holding Aubree's, he flattened his on her back in the same way he had on Aubree's.

"When I tell you to stay somewhere until I come get you, what should you do?" he asked, adjusting his grip on the belt.

"Stay there," Azalea answered after a long pause. Maybe she was considering fighting him on the punishment. He'd hoped seeing Aubree take her spanking so easily, she would accept hers as well. Ten strokes, at least while Aubree was in the room.

"Why didn't you?" he asked glancing at Aubree. She had focused on Azalea, holding her and giving what support she could.

"I—" she sighed. "I don't know."

Not entirely true, but he would explore it with her later. Aubree was a stranger, and he wouldn't force Azalea to spill her guts before her.

"Not really an answer, but I don't want to keep Aubree here all day while you try to elaborate." He patted her bottom, enjoying the slight bounce of her cheek. "Here we go. Ten." He didn't bother telling her to keep quiet. She either would out of sheer stubbornness, or she'd be unable to hold back the noise. He needed more time to train her.

Time. A concept he had no desire to contemplate at the moment.

She jolted with the first strike and stiffened with the second.

"Soften this ass, Azalea." He tapped the folded end of the belt against her cheeks.

Once her muscles relaxed, he laid down the third and fourth swats of the belt. She didn't make any noise, stubborn girl, but she did put her legs out straight behind her to clench once more.

He simply slapped the back of her thighs until she lowered them. "Don't do that again, or you'll have ten more belt lashes across your thighs," he warned. Aubree looked up at him with his threat, but quickly concentrated on Azalea again, whispering something into her ear that he couldn't make out.

"I asked you to hold her hands, not give her sympathy through her punishment," he reprimanded sharply.

"Sorry," Aubree muttered and pinched her lips together.

With a nod, he went back to the job before him. Azalea hadn't turned back to look at him when he spoke. He brushed her hair from her back, letting it curtain around her face.

Another brush of his hand across her naked flesh, and he was ready to begin again.

He brought the leather down, over and over again, counting the strokes in his head. Watching them fall onto her round buttocks and create the red lines across her ass made his balls tighten in his slacks.

Azalea lifted her legs again after a hard swat to the sweet upcurve of her ass but quickly dropped them. She still hadn't said a word, but her grunts were getting more pronounced.

"Do you think you can manage to stay where I ask you to, or will I have to start tying you down?" he asked, the last strike ready to be delivered.

He heard a sniffle, soft and gentle—much like her—before she spoke.

"Yes." Another small sniffle. "Sir."

He darted his gaze to her, expecting to see the back of her head, but instead, finding her staring over her shoulder at him, her eyes shimmering from unfallen tears. Could she be teasing him at the end of her punishment?

No. There wasn't any merriment in that gaze. She wasn't a manipulator; he doubted she knew the skill at all.

Pulling back, he unleashed the last—and hardest—of the

lashes across both ass cheeks. She cried out but didn't move, just dropped her head, her shoulders shaking without sobs.

Aubree brushed back Azalea's hair from her face and wiped the tears from her cheeks. The scene so sweet, so arousing, Peter almost wished he could break his rule about playing with the Annex girls.

"Aubree, you're finished here. Tommy will be sure to get you on the roster tonight at whichever club you choose."

She nodded and climbed off the couch, giving Azalea one more pat to her shoulder before she made her way from the room.

He stood behind Azalea still, watching her as she pressed her hands to the couch cushions, waiting for his instruction.

"You aren't finished." He laid a hand to her ass, enjoying the tremble going through it.

CHAPTER 13

Azalea watched the last tear drop to the leather beneath her. Her bottom lip hurt from biting down on it while Peter delivered the fiery strapping. It hadn't been worse than her first, but he definitely made his point. Having another woman there, watching, hadn't worsened the experience as she first feared when she realized what Peter meant to do. In fact, having Aubree hold her gave her some comfort.

She slid backward, trying to get her feet on the floor, but he cupped her ass, stilling her.

"Not yet," he said as he gripped her flesh, his fingertips digging into her sore bottom.

"Peter, I'm sorry." Maybe an apology would move this along. Her backside hurt, and if she squeezed her legs together she could feel her own arousal collecting. She needed to get away from him and take care of the problem. "I'll leave you alone while you work."

He released her but didn't take his touch away from her. The warmth of his skin on her already-hot bottom sank into her, making her clit tingle.

"Remember last night when I said we'd talk about honesty this morning?" He moved his hand in circles around her ass.

"Yeah, I remember. I didn't lie to you this morning," she pointed out, trying to look over her shoulder at him, but all her damn hair was in the way.

"You didn't exactly answer me, though, either. So, we're going to work on that, now. I'm going to ask you a question and if you answer honestly, you'll be rewarded. If you lie, even a tiny bit, I'll reapply the belt."

The game sounded easy enough, but so far nothing with Peter had been what it seemed.

"I want to know why, exactly, you tried to stop me from punishing Aubree." His hand stilled, like he was giving her his full undivided attention.

"Do I have to be hanging upside down for this?" she asked, needing another moment to think before answering.

"Deflection is a form of dishonesty," he said, and she clenched her ass, waiting for the belt to descend on her again. But it didn't come. Instead, he helped her back over the couch to her feet and brushed her hair away from her face.

"Get out of these jeans and sweater and climb up on the desk. On all fours," he directed her. The room must have been used for the purpose of discipline; there was nothing on the desk. No file cabinets, no telephone anywhere. Just a large mahogany desk with one chair and the couch with a coffee table in the room.

She didn't hesitate to obey him, glad he hadn't taken the opportunity to strap her again.

Once she climbed up, feeling the unforgiving, cool wood press against her bare knees, she tried to see him again. But he was behind her, his fingers trailing down her spine and over her ass.

"You have a few welts, and I think this one will bruise." He pressed into the sensitive spot. She hissed at the horrible sensation.

He draped the leather belt over her back and slipped a hand between her clenched thighs. He wiggled his hand and pinched her thighs until she spread her legs. He could have simply told her to open them, but she was sure he enjoyed it more this way.

"Why did you try to stop the punishment for Aubree?" he asked while dragging a fingernail up and down her inner thigh, almost touching her arousal, yet too far away to satisfy her.

"I—" she huffed. She couldn't admit she'd been sitting in the office thinking about him touching someone else and felt a pain in her chest. No, she was not going to tell him she had even an ounce of jealousy for what he was going to do.

"Did you think I was going to harm her?" He dug his nail deeper into her flesh.

"No." Of that she'd been sure. When he'd strapped her for trying to escape, he'd been hard on her, he'd hurt her, but he hadn't harmed her.

"Did you think she didn't deserve the punishment?" His fingers brushed her pussy lips as he moved to her other thigh.

"I didn't know what she'd done wrong, so—I guess not." She closed her eyes when he pinched her again.

"Good girl. See? This is going well." He lightly tapped her clit. "Fuck, you're wet, Azalea," he said running his thumb through her folds. "Here, see?" Leaning over her, he presented his thumb for her view.

Glistening with her juices, the proof was right in front of her eyes. She swallowed, trying to ignore the bit of embarrassment welling inside her.

"Clean my finger, Azalea," he ordered, bringing it to her

lips. She couldn't do that, not like this, displayed on all fours on a desk.

"Remember, good behavior comes with rewards." He wiggled his thumb. He enjoyed her humiliation too much.

She opened her mouth and took his finger inside, licking off the sweet flavoring of her juices. He pulled it out of her closed lips, creating a *pop.*

"Good girl." He pet her head, down her back, and to her ass. "Did you want to watch her get her spanking?"

She shook her head. A sound swat to her ass answered her.

"No, I didn't want to watch." Though she would admit to herself, that being next to Aubree while she'd received her belting had been more arousing than she would have guessed. Hearing her little gasps, the leather snapping against her upturned ass, the feel of the breeze as the belt whizzed through the air before making contact on the other woman's backside had all heightened her senses and aroused state.

"Did you not want me touching someone else? Were you —jealous?"

Fuck him for coming up with that question. If she lied, he would know right off, and she'd be getting that damn belt again instead of the pleasurable fondling. And she was too hot not to be touched by him.

She sighed. He already knew the truth. All his other questions had just been an opportunity to drag out the session and make her believe she wouldn't have to admit to the real reason.

"I-it seemed strange. I didn't like it." It was as close to admitting the jealousy as she would come.

"Ah." He slipped a finger into her pussy. Her answer must have pleased him. She lowered her lashes, biting down hard on her tongue, trying not to moan with the delicious feeling of his finger inside of her.

"And was it worth getting your ass belted, too?" he asked while sliding a second digit into her.

"Hmmm." She nodded.

"I see," he said and pulled away from her. "How does someone who was sheltered as much as you were have so many dirty thoughts and fantasies?" He grabbed her ass.

She wasn't sure how to answer that question. She hadn't thought about it before.

He spread her ass cheeks wide, and she crawled a bit forward.

"No, you stay put," he admonished. "This little pucker here—" He pressed a fingertip to the spot she hadn't even touched. "I think after I've fucked your pussy, I'll fuck this, too. And your mouth. I'll use every hole your body has to offer. And you'll become even more jealous at the thought of me touching another woman."

She squeezed her eyes closed, promising her body anything it could possibly want if it would just stop responding to his crude words.

"You got wet while I was spanking Aubree." He leaned forward and swiped his tongue over her asshole. She whined but didn't move. That shouldn't have felt as good as it did.

"You enjoyed hearing her little gasps, seeing the belt cross her ass. If you had seen how pretty her cheeks bounced, I think you would have touched yourself."

She tried to block out his words, but he wouldn't be ignored.

She heard a suckling sound and a pop right before she felt his wet finger pushing against her asshole again. She clenched down, but he smacked her hard.

"Submit everything, Azalea," he reminded her again of her promise. "Relax and breathe."

She fisted her hands.

"You're going to come like this, with my finger in your ass."

"I was honest. I didn't lie."

"Don't mistake this for a punishment. This will teach you a different lesson. Pleasure comes in all sorts of ways. Be quiet while I fuck your ass and your pussy with my fingers."

Her thighs tightened, and she thought of lunging off the desk, but when two of his fingers reentered her pussy, she found herself leaning forward, resting her forehead on the desk, and allowing him more access to her body.

So fucking full. And good, and warm. He pumped in and out of both her openings. Her breath picked up; her heart raced.

"Soaking wet, my little hideaway slut."

His words could have been fucking her as well, with the way her body reacted to them. She was acting like a slut. On all fours, her ass in the air, letting him touch her the way he was.

A dirty little slut.

"Come for me, Azalea. Come hard for me, and don't you dare be quiet about it. I want to hear your screams." He pumped harder and faster, and she found herself backing into him, fucking his fingers as much as he was fucking her.

"Oh. Oh. Fuck," she chanted, gripping the sides of the desk and gyrating against him.

"Such a beautiful red ass," he praised, curling his fingers inside her pussy. "Such a naughty girl you were, but now you'll be good. You'll be my little slut and come."

"Oh fuck!" She lurched backward at him. A small touch, maybe his pinkie, to her clit set off all the rockets in her body, and she screamed. She yelled his name, she cursed, she praised the heavens, she lost track of language and time, and she simply rode his fingers, feeling the burn in her ass, the pulsations in her pussy until the very last tingle of her orgasm faded away.

With a huff, she collapsed forward again, her cheek pressed against the warm wood.

His fingers slid out of her body, and he spoke soothingly. She heard him, and on some level understood him, but he sounded so far away. Somewhere above her, or behind her, she couldn't tell anymore.

She gently lowered her body to the desk, rolling to her side and pulling her knees to her chest. Her heart rate slowed, and her breathing came easier, but she couldn't find her focal point. Was he still in the room?

"I think we found your button." His voice came again, lighthearted and soft.

"I—" She tried to wet her lips, but her tongue was dry; her mouth was dry. Her pussy was still wet from her arousal and her orgasm. She'd come so hard. With his fingers in her ass.

"Shhh." He pulled her to sitting and wrapped a robe around her shoulders, helping her arms through the holes. "I'll get you some water when we get upstairs," he promised and tied the robe closed at her stomach. Where'd it come from?

She nodded, unsure of what she'd say if she tried to speak.

He lifted her effortlessly and cradled her to his chest. She wrapped her arms around his neck and let him take her wherever he wanted. She vaguely heard him speak to a few people they passed along the way but didn't register much of it.

She recognized his bed once she was placed on it, feeling the softness and inhaling his scent. True to his word, he gave her some water then helped her beneath the covers—after removing the robe.

He seemed to keep her naked whenever possible.

"Sleep, Azalea. Don't leave my suite until I come for you," he ordered.

Was he continuing her punishment, or was he testing her? She didn't know, and her eyelids were too heavy for her to take the time to inspect the thoughts.

She felt his lips, warm and thick, press against her cheek, and then he was gone. Only a soft click of the door signaled she was alone.

Except she could still feel the burn of his belt on her ass, the stretch of his fingers inside her, and the warmth of his kiss on her cheek.

No. She wasn't alone.

CHAPTER 14

"Peter." Hunter, a former client of the Annex, rose from his chair in the office with an extended hand.

Peter took it in greeting. "What brings you back here? Is Jae giving you too much trouble?" Peter joked. Jaelynn had been contracted from a party to Hunter for a weekend, but she never returned—becoming his full-time submissive.

"She will never be too much trouble." Hunter grinned. "Just the right amount."

Peter laughed. He understood the sentiment.

"So, what brings you around?" Peter sat across the desk.

"I heard you've been looking for a man named Santos." Hunter leaned forward in his seat.

"I am," Peter said with a firm nod.

"He's been to see my uncle," Hunter said. "My uncle has some dealings with Santos's boss. Santos came looking for help. Says you have his boss's daughter." Hunter leaned back, leaving the sentence open in the air.

"I do." Peter gave another nod. "And if he's got any balls

on him, he'll come to talk to me, not your damn uncle about it."

Hunter opened his hands as though to ward off an argument. "You know how I feel about my uncle's dealings, but you also know there's little I can do about it right now. He wants to know if you have her, and if so, he'd like you to turn her over to me so I can bring her home."

Peter laughed. "That's not going to happen. Did Santos also inform your uncle he owed Ashland over a hundred grand?"

Hunter shook his head. "I'm sure he left that out."

"The girl stays with me. When her mother returns from whatever trip she's on, she can come collect her, but I will not hand her over to fucking Santos."

"So, she's not being sold?" Hunter raised his brows.

"We don't sell the unwilling. You know that," Peter ground out.

"I know, I know. That's why I offered to come speak to you. Didn't seem right, you just taking the girl from her home. That's not how things are done here anymore."

Azalea hadn't been given a choice in the matter of coming home with him, but Peter wasn't going to explain the events to Hunter.

"When her mother comes back—"

"That's what has Santos all in a fucking uproar. Her mother is probably going to have his head for letting her out of his sight. I don't understand the whole thing. Last I saw of Bellatrix Gothel, she never mentioned a kid. Even my uncle was surprised to hear of it, and he'd been dealing with her for years."

"Dealing with her, how? I can't imagine she works on his garbage routes or in that casino of his. She seems older, more along the lines of his age—"

"No, nothing like that. I believe she's a supplier." Hunter's gaze faltered. They both knew what a supplier in Jansen's world meant. And it wasn't any product that could be stored on a shelf.

"I've heard her name before, but I can't place her. If she's a big supplier, Samuel would have mentioned her, right? I would have seen her around the house growing up. Maybe Ash remembers her." Peter rubbed his chin. "She never mentioned a kid at all? She had two daughters. One was kidnapped."

"My uncle said he didn't know much about her. She's very quiet about her work, doesn't like to be out in the open. Maybe she never mentioned her kids because she kept business away from family. I remember your father once coming over to my uncle's when I was in high school. He mentioned her—I only remember because it's such an odd name. But I don't ever remember seeing her or hearing of her otherwise."

Peter's stomach clenched at the mention of his father. He'd made the ultimate sacrifice to keep business from hurting his family, taken a bullet aimed at Peter during a bad deal.

"So, she may have worked with Samuel then, too." Peter forced his thoughts to stick to the topic at hand. Wandering off thinking about the past never gained anything. "I have my men looking into her, but I'll have them check the old records again. Maybe Samuel has her marked somewhere as a vendor."

"Thought he filled his own inventory," Hunter said with a huff.

"Most of the time, yeah, but he wasn't averse to buying from the outside. And if I remember correctly, your uncle preferred the quick sale."

Hunter nodded. It didn't matter what vocabulary they used, neither of the men liked the business practices of their families. The buying and selling of women was a bit more complex, a bit more gut twisting than simply ordering stock and having it delivered like they were in the market for party supplies.

"You don't think this girl you have held up here is one of hers, do you?" Hunter stood from his chair, buttoning his jacket.

The thought hadn't occurred to him, and now that it had, there was no fucking way she was leaving with her mother until Peter had every damn question answered to his satisfaction.

"I'm sure it's not the case," Hunter said when Peter didn't remark. "I'll give my uncle your response."

"Remind him that I protect what's mine, and until her mother returns and Azalea decides otherwise, the girl is mine." Peter kept his tone firm and didn't bat an eye as he ground his glare into Hunter.

"I will," Hunter said with a nod. Peter had no quarrel with him. He had the same struggle Ash and Peter had with Samuel. Blood made them family and created a loyalty that couldn't be broken. Until Hunter could take over as the head of his family, little would change.

"And tell your wife we all said hello." Peter broke out of his tense demeanor as he pulled the door open for Hunter. "She's welcome to come by anytime to visit. I know a few of the girls have mentioned wanting to see her."

"She's not setting foot in the Annex ever again," Hunter said with finality. "But if you'd let them meet in the gardens or the main house, I'll bring her over once all this mess with Bellatrix is over."

"That would be fine." Peter nodded. "A little afraid she'd miss the place if she went inside?" he teased.

Hunter's jaw tensed. "No. Afraid I'll remember she used to work there and have to kill you for letting another man touch her."

Peter laughed. "I was one of those men, you realize." Jaelynn didn't take to rules any easier than most of the girls when they first arrived at the Annex. He'd had the job of disciplining her on more than one occasion.

Hunter deadpanned. "I've done an extremely good job at blocking that part of her life out of my mind. Don't make me regret that."

"Okay, okay." Peter slapped him on the back. He knew when to break the teasing, and Hunter's murderous glare gave the cue it was time to stop.

Peter stepped out into the hall with Hunter. A man, not much older than himself, walked up to them, with Johnny right behind him.

"Damien. This is Peter Titon. Peter, this is Damien. He's my right hand."

Damien's hair was cropped excessively short, but Peter could still easily make out the stark blond coloring. And his eyes. He knew those eyes.

Shaking himself out of his suspicions, he took Damien's outreached hand and shook it. "Did Johnny give you the tour?" he asked nodding toward the doors leading to the playrooms.

"Yeah, he did. I've never been to one of your catalogue parties, but I wouldn't mind an invite." He grinned. "Since Hunter's not utilizing your services any longer."

Peter couldn't help but stare. The resemblance was too clear, too uncanny.

"Yeah, I'm sure we can do that." Johnny spoke when Peter continued to remain silent.

"Great." Damien gave Johnny a puzzled look but nodded all the same.

Hunter cut off the staring contest and said his goodbyes.

Peter made the right movements, shook hands, nodded,

said the appropriate goodbyes, but his mind was already swirling.

Once they were gone, Johnny brought him out of his thoughts. "You saw that, right?"

"The resemblance?"

"Yeah. That can't be a coincidence, right? I mean how many people have that color hair?"

Peter agreed. Not many from his suspicion. "Where's Azalea?"

"In your room. She took your laptop up there. I figured since you let her on it in the office, it was okay."

"Yeah, it's fine. Have you found anything on her mother? Any deals she may have had with Samuel?"

Johnny shifted his weight. "No. But his coding is so old, it could be right there, and I wouldn't know."

"Yeah." Just another way his uncle kept such tight control.

"What about this Damien. Did you get a last name?"

"No. But I can get one. I'll look into him today."

"And I want you to look into a kidnapping of a preteen girl with the last name of Gothel. Probably about twenty years ago," Peter said.

If Johnny had more questions, he wasn't asking them.

"You got it. Daniel's out on a collection, and the girls have three appointments this afternoon. Are you going over to Tower?"

"I haven't decided yet," Peter said. "Other than getting Daniel up to speed, don't tell anyone about Damien."

"Got it."

"Good. I'm going to find Azalea, and I don't want to be disturbed."

CHAPTER 15

*A*zalea sprawled across the massive bed on her stomach, working on the laptop. Things would be moving faster if she had her own computer with her—she already had the programs she needed—but she would have to make do for the time being.

The door to the bedroom pushed open, and she glanced to be sure it was Peter and not one of his men. She hadn't had any issues with them, and they gave her the impression Peter had warned them away from her, but she still didn't trust them.

"What are you up to?" Peter asked in his low tone that sent a tingle through her.

"I have been working on increasing your revenue," she announced proudly. It occurred to her that he could be upset with her meddling, but he needed her help.

He just didn't know it yet.

"Oh yeah? And how have you done that?" he asked with skepticism.

She pushed up from her position and sat with her legs crossed, flipping the computer around to show him. "I've made new graphics—well, a few—for your website and then I spruced up the site to give it a better look."

He leaned over the bed, pressing his hands into the mattress to examine the screen. She hadn't changed much, only the entire color scheme.

"How the hell did you get access to the website?" he asked, still looking over what she'd done. He didn't sound angry, but sometimes she couldn't tell without seeing his eyes.

"Well, you didn't pick a very secure password, and it auto-populated your email address." She shrugged. "It wasn't hard. But, you may want to pick a harder password than Tower."

He moved his gaze from the computer screen to her. Dark eyes, but not quite the usual storm. She'd probably pricked his ego but hadn't quite pissed him off.

"You changed the colors."

"They match the actual club now. You have a lot of gold and black there; it's a very sensual atmosphere. I made the site match. And the graphics—you had some casual stock photos. I jazzed them up a bit." She pointed to the home page. What was once just empty tables in a nightclub, now had images from the actual club, a few of them taken of the live art in the catacombs of the main room.

"Where'd you get the photos?" he asked, scrolling through the website.

"You had them on your hard drive." She crawled to him and peeked over the monitor. "It's still a little rough, but I don't have my computer with my programs, so I had to use the open-source stuff I got online."

"Where'd you learn to do all this?" he asked, standing up.

She looked up at him. "School. I have a degree in graphic design. But the website stuff I learned on my own."

"Your mother let you go to school? I would have thought she'd homeschool you."

"When I was young, she did. Well, not her—I had tutors. But when I finished high school, she let me enroll in college. Santos or one of her other men was always with me, but at least she let me go." She didn't mean to sound as though her mother had completely locked her away and forgotten about her, even if it had sometimes felt that way growing up.

"Hmmm. You said you had an older sister. Do you remember her?"

Azalea shook her head. "No. Mother had me after she was abducted."

"Ever see a picture of her?"

"Just a few. When she was young, like two or three maybe." Azalea hadn't pressed too hard for details about her older sister. Her mother had become so distraught and paranoid at any reminder of the loss of her daughter, she would force Azalea to remain her room for days at a time. Not chancing someone being able to kidnap her as well, she insisted. Azalea learned not to bring it up if she didn't want the door of her suite locked.

"Any brothers?" he asked.

What was he fishing for?

"No. Why are you asking me all this?" Azalea slid off the bed. "Did something happen? Have you found Santos?"

Peter laughed. "No. Nothing like that." He went to his closet and shrugged out of his jacket, hung it up, and unbuttoned the sleeves of his shirt.

"Do you hate the website?" she asked, glancing back at it.

"No. I love it, actually. You did an amazing job. In fact, I think I'll put you in charge of all the advertising and website design."

"I don't know very much about advertising," she admitted.

"Well, then maybe we should sign you up for some classes

at the college." A lock of hair fell in front of his forehead, giving him a soft, wistful look.

"But I'm only going to be here another week or two," she said softly.

"We don't know that."

"You promised," she reminded with force.

"I promised when your mother came, we'd discuss it. You may not want to leave when the time comes. Have you thought of that?" He finished rolling his left sleeve up to his elbow and made his way to her. With each predatory step he took, she backpedaled, until her legs were pressed against the bed.

"You're not mad about the website, are you?" she asked softly, feeling his body even though he hadn't actually touched her yet.

"No. I mean—you really shouldn't be snooping in my computer, and even if it's easy to hack an account, you shouldn't. But since I benefited, I'll leave it be." Using both hands, he pushed her hair behind her.

"What are you doing, then?" she asked, daring to look up at him.

"Making sure you won't want to leave when the time comes." He brought his mouth down on hers, unyielding while he framed her face. She lost herself easily in the kiss. He nibbled her lower lip, and she arched into him, wanting more. More sweetness of his caressing tongue, more pain from the sharpness of his teeth. She wanted both, and she needed them more.

When he ended the kiss, she looked at him through a haze of arousal and need. When had this man become less of an asshole and more of something she craved?

"You think a little kiss will do that?" she teased but didn't lift her gaze to his. Eye-to-eye contact would make her lose her nerve, and she'd spent too much time calculating this to begin with.

"Hmm, is my girl getting greedy already?" He pulled at the T-shirt she wore. "Take this damn thing off. I thought I had Daniel bring you some real clothes."

"He did, but I wanted something comfortable, not all those dresses."

Peter paused in his tugging of her shirt over her head. "So, where'd you get this, then?" he asked, yanking it off her and shaking it at her.

"It's Aubree's. She gave me a few things," Azalea said.

His jaw ticked. "You spoke with Aubree?"

"You didn't say I couldn't talk with people. In fact, you said I could go anywhere on the estate. I haven't tried to run away, and I didn't even go in your precious Annex."

"I didn't say you did anything wrong. I'm just surprised."

"What? That I know how to be sociable?" He must have thought her mother kept her under lock and key. Which, of course, she had, but Azalea had learned at a decent age how to get out from under that suffocating thumb of her mother's and have some friendly encounters.

"I didn't say that."

She tried to push away from him, but he grabbed her arm and pulled her right back in place.

"Then stop looking so pissed," she demanded, grabbing the shirt from him and covering her naked bosom with it.

"This isn't my pissed face, Azalea." He gingerly took the garment from her and dropped it to the floor. "I don't want to talk about clothes anymore, or social conversations, what I want is your body naked, sprawled out on my bed." He reached around her and snagged the laptop, shutting it. "Make that happen."

"Make that happen?" she laughed. "Like I'm one of your employees?"

"No." He turned his dark stare on her. "Like you're a good girl who doesn't want to end up with a spanking instead of a fucking."

Her jaw dropped.

"But—"

He closed in on her space, gripping both of her nipples and pulling them toward him until she cried out, and then he lessened the stretch.

"*But* nothing. I'm making you mine, Azalea."

She whimpered when he released her. The return of the blood flow to her nipples stung, and she tried to rub it away. He swatted her hands away.

"You never cover yourself from me." His words were hard, like he wanted to be sure she knew he meant business, that he was the one holding the reins, and she could either comply or be punished. And she'd seen how much he loved to punish.

She had no doubt he would switch to the paddle instead of thinking of sex if she resisted him.

And did she really want to resist him? Hadn't she already decided that afternoon while she worked on his business that she wanted him to take her? She wanted every part of her to be touched by him. Even if they were only together for a short time. Even if she was going back home with her mother when she arrived. To have that memory. To feel his desire for her, to sense the urgency and know she gave him everything. She could live on that memory for a long time.

"If I say no?" she asked, already toying with the hems of the black leggings.

"I've never forced a woman," he replied, his expression stone cold.

It wasn't much of an answer, but what had she expected? Even if he had forced a woman, would he cop to it? Would he tell her the truth?

In their time together, as far as she was aware, he'd never lied to her. Studying him, she looked for a crevice in his honesty, a crack in that stern exterior. Nothing.

"Are you saying no, Azalea?" His voice was husky.

"Shouldn't a girl's first time be…I don't know…" She felt her cheeks heat at the implication. She was going to say *special*, but what did that even mean?

He gave a low laugh. "Want me to spread rose petals all over the bed for you? Light a few candles? Maybe write you a quick sonnet?"

"No." And she didn't. She couldn't imagine it being that way with him. With all his sharp edges and dark glares, he'd look out of place. It would be—wrong.

"You're mine, now, Azalea. And I always take care of what's mine. Always." He inched closer to her, taking away what little space stood between them.

She believed him. Even when her mind rebelled and told her she shouldn't be giving over to him. She never should have agreed to play his little game and let him own her for the short time they were together. Even if he offered everything she wanted, she should have held firm and told him to fuck off.

But she would never get to do anything in her life if she always listened to that horrible voice in her head telling her to be good, to do what she was supposed to do and lay low.

"You're still dressed," he said, pulling the elastic of her leggings away from her stomach then snapped it back in place.

Hooking her thumbs into the band, she pushed them down to her ankles, bumping her head on his chest as she bent over slightly. He didn't back up, didn't give her room, simply stood his ground.

Like always.

Like she'd come to expect from him.

Once she managed to step out of the leggings, she shoved them to the side. Not sure where to put her hands, she clasped them together behind her, figuring if she covered her sex he'd slap them away.

"Very good," he whispered, trailing the tips of his fingers over her collarbone. "Get on the bed, Azalea," he ordered.

She took a deep breath and pushed herself up onto the bed, scooting back as far as the headboard would allow her. As much as she wanted him, wanted him to be her first, she had a bubble of fear in her belly.

When he touched her, it was easy to forget how experienced he was. She didn't think about all the other women he'd been with or who he would be with once she was gone. When he touched her, looked into her eyes, he made her unable to think about anything other than him.

But now, watching him shed his clothes, even with his focus on her, she knew she'd fail at this. She knew he'd probably find her lacking and naive—just like he did in every other avenue of life. She would always be the sheltered girl who knew nothing because her mother cared too much about her to let her live a normal life.

"Azalea." He called her name firmly, and she dragged her gaze to his face. A wrinkle of concern creased his brow, but his eyes remained stoic. "Stop overthinking. There's nothing to think about here."

He shoved his slacks down, let them fall to his feet, and his cock sprang free.

She reached for him, to touch his length, his strength, but he caught her wrist and shook his head. "No."

He climbed up on the bed, pushing her thighs apart like he had before, and moved down to his elbows. He brought his mouth to her clit, licking, flicking then sucking.

Her stomach clenched, and her breath caught.

More licking, slow and treacherous before the sharp bite of his teeth.

"Fuck." She let out a breath.

He gave a low laugh. "Such naughty words." He bit down on the inside of her thigh.

He spread her legs open wider, moved up her figure, and kissed her mouth. It felt good having his naked body against hers, the warmth, the strength of him pressing her to the mattress.

His cock touched her entrance, and she tensed.

"Shh, don't get all wound up on me. It will make it worse," he said between kisses.

His hands roamed her body, feeling her curves, her tits, and tweaking her nipples while his tongue did things that made her mind blank.

"Your pussy is soaked," he said against her mouth. "My cock is already wet with your juices."

Again, her cheeks heated from the humiliating way her body reacted to him.

"Why is your pussy so wet, Azalea?" he asked, pausing in his kisses to stare down at her.

When she tried to turn away, he caught her face with both hands and held her steady. "Why?"

"You're an asshole," she said. He got off on making her acutely aware of every fucking sensation, every pleasurable thing he did to her.

Yeah, a complete asshole.

He laughed. "Tell me." He shifted, making the tip of his cock press harder against her entrance. Another move like that, and he'd be inside her.

She didn't want him to plunge inside and feed the animalistic hunger, she needed it.

"Because I want you." She pressed her hands against his chest, not pushing him, but holding the distance between them.

"See, honesty isn't so hard." He shifted backward, shoving her leg up toward her chest. She'd never been so exposed, felt so vulnerable.

"I want you, too, Azalea," he said, gripping his cock and stroking it. "More than I've wanted a woman in a long time."

Was that his great romantic declaration?

It needed some work.

He ran the head of his cock through her folds before settling at her entrance. He drove forward, stretching her around his thick head.

She curled her fingers into his bare chest, still not forcing him away, but preparing to if needed.

His lips tensed into a straight line, like he was trying hard to keep himself composed and focused.

He thrust, and she yelped.

"Peter," she warned, panic starting to build in her chest. Her pussy stretched around his cock. The sensation pinched, sweeping away her breath. She needed to breathe.

"Azalea," he groaned driving forward again, slow, but not pausing in the least. Another inch—how many had already filled her—and he stopped, leaning back and running his hands down her thigh.

She relaxed her fingers, noticing the small marks her nails made on his pecs.

"Keep your eyes on me, Azalea. Just me, nowhere else," he instructed, still caressing her thighs.

She nodded. Afraid if she opened her mouth, she'd beg him to hurry up and thrust into her. She knew he was trying to save her from the discomfort, but it was the discomfort she craved. If he was going to claim her, claim her, dammit.

She found him beaming down at her, a tilted, cocky smile.

"You like it this way." He edged into her a bit more, grinning wider when she grunted. "You like the stretch and the pain."

"I would like it more if you stopped stopping," she said, feeling much braver now that he was nearly completely inside her. She just needed him to take the plunge, to fill and push and fuck her hard.

He raised an eyebrow. He ran a finger over her clit, rolling it in circles, making her arch her back. The movement took him in farther, and she felt the stretch increase.

Moving over her again, he removed his fingers from her clit and captured her face once more. "Eyes on me, don't even blink," he ordered and thrust hard forward.

She cried out, the pain catching her off guard. "Fuck!" She slapped at his shoulders, pushing him, but not getting him to move.

He stilled over her.

"Relax, your pussy will adjust, just relax," he said and kissed her cheek where a tear had fallen. She took several long breaths, watching him as he relaxed along with her.

The pain ebbed, leaving her with the desire to push up at him, to regain some of the ache. When he slipped a hand between their bodies to play with her clit again, completely wiping away the pain and twisting it into incomparable pleasure, she arched upward.

He pulled back and plowed forward again. She moaned and brought her legs back, opening herself more to him. Wrapping her hands around his back, she held onto him as he fucked her. Slow at first, bringing himself almost all the way out before plunging back in, but once he seemed appeased she wasn't hurting, he fucked her harder.

The bite of pain was back, but pleasure dragged right behind. Every thrust, every buck of his hips drove her to another plane of pleasure.

"Fuck, Azalea, fuck," Peter grunted with a hard drive

forward. His face tightened, his concentration back in full force.

She hauled her legs back further, enjoying the slip in his control when she made the movement.

His fingers rolled around her clit, and he bent lower, kissing her, nibbling on her lower lip.

The burning pressure in her belly building, she planted her feet on the mattress and arched up, taking his cock and wanting more of it.

The bed creaked beneath them.

"Peter." She grabbed him, matching his thrusts with her own.

"Almost there, pretty girl?" he asked, taking her clit between two fingers. "Show me. Show me how pretty my girl is when she comes for me." He squeezed her clit, giving her that extra pinprick while he plowed harder into her, filling her so perfectly.

It was enough to spark the ignition. Her body went off like a bottle rocket.

She screamed—his name, a curse or two, but mostly his name. Over and over, as she bucked up at him, taking every thrust he gave, feeling every bit of his pinch while the waves repeatedly crashed into her.

Just as the electricity died down, he released her clit and grabbed her hips. His jaw clenched, and his fingers dug into her flesh while he pounded his cock into her. Grunts turned into groans.

"Oh fuck," she whispered, feeling his cock thicken inside of her now-sensitive pussy. With one more thrust, he stilled, letting out animalistic moans while his cum filled her.

She watched him unravel, saw the pure emotion of his release as he emptied into her. His breath became harsh, his chest heaved, and after one more drive, he collapsed onto her. His face cradled into her neck, his hot breath washed over her throat.

His arms wrapped around her, holding her tightly to him. She didn't move, didn't push him away, enjoying the weight of him on her. He kissed her neck, shifting to his side and drawing her close. His cock slipped out of her, soiling the bedding beneath her.

But he didn't seem to care, and she lost herself in his embrace.

CHAPTER 16

Peter's phone rang from his back pocket.
"What the hell is going on over there?" Ash's unmistakable voice shot through the phone.
Peter glanced over at Azalea, who sat at a desk in his apartment over Tower working on her laptop. Enough renovations were complete that he could start occupying his own home.
"Hello to you, too," Peter remarked, getting up from his spot on the couch and walking out of the room.
"Why the fuck do you have some woman hostage?" Ash asked.
"She's not a fucking hostage, you ass. Aren't you on your fucking honeymoon?"
"I am. Ellie's taking a nap." As though the mention of his wife was enough to soothe him, Ash's voice lowered. "Tell me what's happening. I call Daniel, and he tells me you have this girl all locked up at the house?"
Peter would have to kill Daniel. "No one's locked up anywhere. Daniel and I went on a collection call, and the guy didn't have the money."

"So you took a girl?" Ash's voice might have been level, but Peter could hear the anger starting to build.

"Yes, but not like you're making it out. She was locked up in her room, Ash."

"So?"

"From the outside. She couldn't walk out if she wanted to. In her own home."

Silence filled the time.

"She's free to leave, now, though?"

Peter ran a hand across his neck. "No, not really. She's staying with me until her mother gets back from business. Then I'll reassess."

"Working foster care?" Ash's tone didn't suggest levity.

"Do you remember a woman named Bellatrix Gothel?" Peter stuck to the facts.

"Yeah. My father dealt with her occasionally. She's a fucking trafficker. I cut her off when I took over. At least three of the girls my father had in the Annex were bought from her. After I released them, I helped return them to their families. Don't you remember?"

"There were a lot of girls we helped find their families, I didn't pay attention to where they'd been purchased." At least a dozen women needed to locate the families that they'd been snatched from by either Samuel Titon's men or other vendors.

"Well, she was one of the vendors. Works pretty low-key, from what I remember. Does a lot of dealings with Jansen, now, I think."

"Yeah. One of her men went to Jansen to get him to intervene on the girl's behalf. Hunter was at the house a few days ago asking me to hand her over."

"And you didn't."

"Fuck, no. I trust Hunter, but no way I'm handing her over to Jansen. When her mother returns—"

"Yeah, yeah, you'll reassess. You think I don't know you? You have no plans to hand that girl back over to her mother."

"You just said she fucking sells women. Why would I—"

"You think she'd sell her own daughter?" Ash cut in.

"Yeah, I do."

More silence stretched out.

"Jansen's not going to like being denied. And Bellatrix isn't a small player, either. She works with families across the country."

"Yeah, all that power, and right now she has no idea her daughter isn't locked up in the damn tower she shoved her into before she left." Peter's ire at the memory of finding that fucking door locked resurfaced.

"What are you going to do with her?"

"I don't know." Peter sighed. It was a question he avoided at every turn.

"Why did you take her? She's an adult. Why not leave her there with the damn door unlocked?" Ash needled.

"Why did you accept Ellie's offer when she showed up at the house?" Peter turned the tables.

Another bout of silence.

"Is this girl your Ellie?"

Now, there was a question.

"My place is almost finished. They are working on the last room this week, so I'll be out of your place by the time you get back, or right after." Exploring his feelings about Azalea, or what the future could bring would not do anyone any good.

"Huh," Ash grunted. "Figures you'd find a girl while I was gone. Just don't marry the woman until I get back."

"You can really be an ass sometimes," Peter hissed.

"I know. My wife tells me all the time. I bet you're being as much of an asshole to your girl—what the hell is her name?"

"Azalea." He tried to keep aloof when saying her name, but he couldn't be sure he didn't sound like some obsessed fan while speaking it.

"Jansen's not going to like being rejected, no matter his nephew is on your side in this. And he's definitely not going to like looking weak when Gothel gets back and finds out he couldn't intervene."

"I'm aware. I have it all handled. You just do whatever the hell you're doing. I'll see you in a few weeks." Peter walked back down the hall to the living room, finding Azalea exactly where he'd left her, at the desk, working.

"You call me if you need me. I'll be on the first flight home." Ash would, too.

"Goodbye, Ash." Peter didn't wait for a response before clicking off the call.

Azalea swiveled around to face him. "Ash. Your cousin?"

"Yeah." Peter said, putting a hand on the back of the office chair and leaning over to kiss her. He couldn't seem to get enough of her taste now that he had her.

"You know, sending me home would solve whatever problems you're having," she said when he broke the kiss.

And just like that, his mood soured.

"How many times have I reminded you of our deal?" he asked, lowering himself to her level.

She bit the corner of her lip.

"How many?"

"Today?" she asked with a saccharine sweetness. He'd warned her to leave the topic alone. Constantly having to remind her what she'd agreed to, what he wanted from her grated on him. Maybe because he couldn't see how he would ever let her go, or maybe because he didn't want to think about it yet. It didn't matter; when he said a subject was off-limits—it was off-fucking-limits.

"Lift the skirt of your dress and bend over the desk." He pushed off the chair.

"Peter."

"Now, or it doubles." He moved into his own position and waited for her. He wouldn't keep being reminded they had a fucking time limit.

He'd rather spend their time together sinking his cock into that tight, hot pussy of hers. And he already had once that morning, but now, he couldn't until they went to bed. Because he didn't fuck punished girls.

Azalea shimmied past him, keeping her ass pointed away from him, and made her way to the front of the desk. Her pleasing look did nothing to sway him, and she seemed to realize faster than usual that she should get in position.

She lifted the hem of the dress to her waist and bent over the desk, raising her round, naked buttocks into the air and placing her palms flat on the desk.

Peter had taken pleasure in teaching her the proper position when being spanked over a desk or table. And she'd enjoyed herself as immensely after having her bottom warmed with his hand and then her pussy fucked hard. But that was playtime.

This was a different kind of lesson.

He pushed her long hair over her shoulders, effectively blocking her view of him. Something she hated, and of course something he would continue to do.

"Tell me again what you agreed to," he said, petting her ass. A soft tremble greeted his touch.

"That I would be yours until my mother came home," she said, not bothering to look back at him. It would be useless anyway.

"That's right. And are you allowed to keep asking me to take you home?"

"No, sir."

His balls tightened at the three-letter word she'd tacked onto her answer.

"And yet you've mentioned it four times today." The other three had been random comments about how to keep his website up to date after she went home. But they counted.

"So, I think that means you owe me four."

He stepped closer to her, wrapping his arm around her slender waist and pulling her against his body.

"Okay," she said with a little more sarcasm than he should allow.

The poor thing thought he meant four spanks.

She jolted when his fingers slipped between her legs and through her folds, gathering the wetness that always seemed to be there when he wanted it. The woman was as aroused as he was at the prospect of punishments.

"Peter?" she asked, trying to crane her neck to see him when he inserted two fingers into her pussy, instantly feeling the clenching flesh.

"Be quiet." He pinched her hip. "When you're done, you can talk—though I doubt you'll be able to." He plunged into her and finger fucked her hard, bending at his knuckles enough to brush against that tender little spot inside of her that drove her crazy.

"Oh. Oh…fuck." She slapped her hand against the desk. "Peter."

Apparently, she wasn't ready to be obedient.

"If you keep talking, I'll have to gag you," he promised.

Squeezing her hard against him, he fucked her fast with his fingers, making sure to brush her clit and drive her to the brink.

"Aaagh." Her body tightened, and she was about to burst.

"Are you going to come?" he asked, not slowing his ministrations.

"Yes! Oh, fuck yes!" She arched her back and gave him better access.

"No, you're not." He plunged in deep, feeling the evidence of the first wave starting, and pulled his hand free, stepping away from her.

He'd heard women cry out in frustration—this wasn't his first punishment, but he'd never heard the raw anger he did with Azalea.

"I probably should have explained. You aren't coming. Bad girls who don't obey don't get to come. But you'll come right up to the edge, right to where you're about to fall into oblivion, and then I'm going to yank you back. Four times. That was number one."

"What? No! Peter!" She tried to get back up, but he planted a hand between her shoulder blades.

Without a word, he wrapped his arm back around her waist and plunged three digits into her. Her head thrown back, she thrust her ass toward him.

He listened to her moans, felt her body's reaction as he curled his fingers, stroked the right spots. She settled into soft moans.

Cute girl. She thought she could sneak an orgasm.

"Are you going to come?" he asked, looking at the back of her head. She shook it, probably knowing if she opened her mouth, the truth would spill out.

"Good." He again backed away as her pussy clamped down on his fingers extra hard.

Another guttural muttering and a smack to the desk.

"That's two," he said, his breath somewhat labored from the ministrations.

Deciding to give his fingers a break, he squatted behind her, pulling her ass cheeks far apart.

"Peter, what—oh fuck." She wiggled, but he held her ass cheeks firmly while he licked and teased her pussy. He squeezed the soft flesh of her bottom, giving her nowhere to go.

Fuck, she tasted like heaven. This punishment was worse on him than her, he decided.

The more he licked, the wetter she became. Using the tip of his middle finger, he rimmed her pussy entrance. A deep moan came from him.

Did she realize she was moving her hips? She bucked back at him, taking his tongue inside her.

"Oh fuck," she whispered, thighs trembling on both sides of his head.

Her muscles tightened, and he sat back on his heels, holding her ass cheeks open. Air touched her exposed clit. It was so swollen, so red, so much in need.

"No!" she yelled and stomped her foot.

He laughed. "Three."

"I can't. Please. I can't. I won't mention going home ever again, just please let me come."

He heard the plea in her voice, the tightness and urgency, but it didn't matter. He'd sentenced her, and he would complete the punishment.

"One more, pretty girl. You can do it." He leaned forward again, taking her clit between his teeth and flicking his tongue over it.

She hissed, and he knew it wasn't going to be long before she teetered on the line he would have to drag her away from.

As he suckled her clit, he spread her ass cheeks again, this time, pressing his thumb, wet from her pussy, against the tight ring of her asshole.

She tried to clench, but he shut that down by delivering a hard smack to her ass cheeks and went right back to his objective.

"My finger's going in, Azalea," he said against her pussy

lips and pushed harder until his thumb was inside, up to his knuckle.

"Peter, no," she whispered hoarsely. She said no, but when he thrust two fingers into her pussy, she clamped down and moaned like the needy girl she was.

"Look at you, fingers in your ass and your pussy, moaning like a little slut. Needing an orgasm that won't come because you were so fucking naughty."

She groaned.

"So close, I feel every little tremble." He timed his thrusts so that either her ass or her pussy was being pumped into.

It took no time for her to reach the edge. He played dangerously and kept finger fucking her until he felt the very first tremble of an orgasm before pulling away. She'd feel some waves, the beginning of a weak orgasm would be unleashed, but by the slam of her hand on the desk and the scream of frustration she let loose, it was nowhere near satisfying.

"And that was four. Now, get on your knees." He pulled her dress over her ass and helped her to the floor. When she looked up at him, her hair was wild, her eyes dark and wide.

"Open that pretty mouth," he instructed and unzipped his slacks, pulling his hard-as-fuck cock out.

She licked her lips, the hunger in her eyes changing from needing to be fucked, to needing to feel his cock in her throat.

He would oblige.

Her hot tongue ran under his cock as he slid into her mouth. His hands dove into her hair, clutching at the roots and holding her steady.

"Naughty girls get face fucked, don't they, pretty girl?" He was being rough, and he didn't give a fuck.

Tears built in her eyes as he shoved his thick cock past her lips and farther down until he felt the back of her throat.

She coughed and sputtered, and he pulled back, letting her get a breath, but then he plowed back in, all the way, to the hilt. His balls slapped against her chin.

Fuck. He hadn't thought she'd be able to take all of him. Her throat constricted, she swallowed, and he nearly lost his load then.

She pushed against his thighs. At first, he wanted her to put them behind her back, let him have full control, but he decided to leave them.

Just a bit of a touch. A connection between them.

She didn't fight him, and when she couldn't hold him anymore, he let her breathe.

Once she had air, he plunged back in. Spit poured down her chin, tears ran down her face. She was fucking gorgeous. He held onto her hair, fucking her throat as roughly as he'd fucked her pussy that morning. And she made no complaint.

His balls tightened, his body ready to explode.

"Good girl, pretty slutty, girl," he said between clenched teeth as his release took him over. He retreated enough to see the strings of cum spurt into her mouth. She kept her tongue out, her mouth open, accepting every drop of his seed.

"Arggh" she cried out, her eyes rolling back and closing, but her mouth remained open.

Peter held his cock, stroking it gently, and looked down at her.

She'd come.

She'd fucking had an orgasm while being face fucked.

Her hands had been on his thighs the whole time.

The woman had come without being touched.

He caressed her cheek. "Swallow it all, pretty girl," he instructed when she still had his load resting on her tongue.

She closed her mouth and opened her eyes.

"I know what you did," he said, running his fingers through her hair. "And it was fucking amazing."

"I didn't mean to," she said sheepishly.

"I know." He reached out and helped her stand. "Finish your work and then we'll have lunch." He walked her back around to the chair she'd been sitting in.

"That's it? No nap?" she asked with a raised brow. Typically, he put her to bed after any sort of sexual play.

"Nope. We have to get back to the house this afternoon, and I don't want you working when we do, so finish what you're doing." He tapped the laptop. "Besides, that was supposed to be a punishment." Though he doubted she felt punished at all. Orgasm denial would work with her—he would have to completely deny himself at the same time.

She gathered her hair to one side and quickly braided the long mane, refocusing on her work.

"I just want to make this last image. Maybe you can advertise on social media?"

Peter shrugged. "Whatever you say. It's your thing." He kissed the top of her head and went back to the couch to study the latest financial reports from his accountant.

Or, at least, he could have the papers in front of him while he peeked over and watched her work. He couldn't get enough of her.

CHAPTER 17

Azalea walked through the gardens of Ash's estate. Peter had been taking her to his apartment in the city more and more often, but he always returned to the estate.

Apparently, his cousin would be returning from his honeymoon soon, and business would pick up. She hadn't seen many men show up at the Annex. She'd assumed the women would have playtimes scheduled most evenings, but Peter said a lot of the girls had taken time off while Ash was gone.

Peter had given her a quick tour of the Annex, but still didn't want her wandering around there unless she had an escort. Which she always did. One of his men was always stationed outside his rooms upstairs so if she wanted to explore, she had someone with her.

They never stopped her from roaming, but they were always there. Lurking.

Getting chilled from the crisp air, she headed inside. She could get a little more work done in the office. Peter had given her complete authority in making all the marketing materials for Tower. She'd finished the web design and graphics for social media ads, so all she had to finish were the paper ads. Putting them in kink-friendly magazines would bring in a lot more customers.

The man assigned to watch her wasn't standing inside the doorway anymore. No one was.

Remembering she'd left her laptop—the new one Peter had bought her with all the programs she needed already installed—in the Annex office, she made her way there.

Raised voices greeted her the moment she opened the door to the Annex. Was one of the girls in trouble? Was Peter spanking someone? The sudden surge of jealousy surprised her. She hadn't been so possessive when he punished Aubree, but maybe that was because she'd been there. She and Aubree had gone through it together.

"You don't understand who you're dealing with." A loud voice carried into the hall.

Santos.

She recognized his accent.

Azalea pushed the door to the office open and found the source of all the yelling. Santos was being held back by Tommy, while Peter sat at his desk looking bored.

"What's going on?" Azalea asked, stepping into the room.

"Go back upstairs," Peter said in a firm voice, but he didn't look at her.

"Azalea!" Santos cried out. "Please, tell them you must come home. Your mother will be back in two days. You have to go back." She recognized the panicked expression. Her mother would blame him.

"You've talked with her?" Azalea asked. "Did she ask about me?"

Santos looked at Peter before answering. "She asked if you were home."

"And you lied?" Azalea's heart sank. Her mother rarely

spoke to her while she was away. Busy, busy, busy, she would tell her when she got back. She had no time for little chitchats, but she'd called Santos.

"If she knew you weren't home—" Santos pulled free from Tommy. "Do you know what she'd do to me?"

"If her mother is so scary, why would I let her go back there? You had her locked in her room." Peter stood from his desk, buttoning his jacket.

"Bellatrix is very protective of her daughter." Santos kept his gaze on Azalea, pleading in his eyes. She'd heard her mother yelling at her men before, and she'd heard the whispers of punishments her mother doled out to them.

When she was a young girl, she'd walked in on her mother slapping one of her men across the face. Her complexion had been red and angry, her eyes wild with rage. When she'd noticed Azalea in the room, she took a slow breath and plastered a soft smile on her lips. It wasn't real. Even as a girl, Azalea knew what a fake smile looked like. Bellatrix had sent her to her room, telling her Mommy had important work to do. And as soon as Azalea stepped inside her suite, she'd heard the resounded lock of the bolt.

"My mother isn't kind to those who work for her," Azalea agreed. Santos would be punished for letting Peter take her from home. "He has good reason to be afraid of her."

Peter raised both eyebrows and gave her a pointed look. "The same mother you insist loves you so much, she's been keeping you locked away out of fear of losing you?"

Azalea nodded. "She's never raised a hand to me, Peter." Or wrapped her arms around her in a loving embrace, but Azalea had grown used to her mother's unique ways of showing her affection. An extra bit of dessert on her dinner tray or an extra hour at the playground in the evening—with one of her men standing guard.

Peter focused on Santos again. "Were you working for Bellatrix when Azalea was born?"

Santos flicked his gaze to Azalea then back to Peter. "I was a boy. My father worked for her when Azalea came —was born."

Peter folded his arms over his chest. "How old were you?"

"I was ten, I think." Santos's shoulders rolled back and forth again, like his skin felt too tight all of a sudden.

"Do you remember her father?"

"Azalea's?" Santos looked to her, again with a silent plea for her to intervene. But she wanted to know the answer, too. She'd never bothered asking him. Her mother had made it clear her father wasn't around and never would be—and not to keep asking about him.

"Do you?" Peter pressed.

"N-no. I was a kid." Santos's voice wavered, a smidgen, right at the beginning.

"Didn't Jansen tell you what my decision was?" Peter asked, moving closer to Santos. The two men who'd been holding him flanked him but kept their hands off. Ready to jump in if needed.

"She won't accept that." Santos shook his head.

Peter gave a low laugh. He wasn't happy, no, this laugh made her spine chill. This man, stalking toward Santos, wasn't the same who'd climbed into bed with her the night before.

Peter reached behind him and pulled out a gun, Azalea had never seen him carry one before. Or was it always there in hiding beneath his suit jacket.

He pressed the barrel up against Santos's forehead. Azalea froze. Would he shoot him? Right there in front of her in the office?

"I don't give a fuck what Bellatrix Gothel will accept or

not accept. If she wants to ask Azalea to go home, she'll come here when she gets back in town. And we'll talk about it. But Azalea is not leaving with you."

Santos winced as Peter pushed the gun harder against his head. Small beads of sweat lined his forehead and temple; his hands shook at his sides.

Shouldn't she speak up? Say something?

"Get the fuck out of here, and if you go crying to anyone else, or show your ugly face here again, you won't be given the courtesy of leaving in one piece." Peter pulled back, holding the gun at his side and keeping his glare fixed on Santos.

"When Mother gets home, tell her I'm safe. Tell her that I want to see her here, okay? Tell her I left on my own—"

"No." Peter's voice acted as a foot stomping onto the ground. "No, you tell her the damn truth. That your fucking debt got her in this mess. That when it came time to pay up, I took Azalea. You tell her you didn't stop it, you stood there while I walked out of that house with Azalea."

Santos swallowed, his jaw working but nothing being said. Finally, after a long pause, he nodded. "I'll bring her here."

"We'll be waiting," Peter announced walking over to Azalea and pulling her to his side with his gun back in his pants. "Take Mr. Santos to his car, and be sure he gets home safe," Peter said to his men, who both nodded mutely and gave Santos a shove.

Santos looked over his shoulder once more before being pushed out the door, giving Azalea a hard glare. He blamed her. It didn't matter that he'd gotten them both into the mess with whatever he did to have such a debt. It didn't matter that she hadn't gone willingly with Peter in the first place. The only thing that mattered was that once again, she'd caused trouble.

"She'll be home in two days?" Azalea broke the silence, putting space between her and Peter. In two days, she would be back in her own room, in her own bed, under her own roof. No, her mother's roof.

Everything there belonged to her mother. Azalea owned nothing, had nothing there. She'd resided in that house, but she hadn't actually lived there.

Looking across the room at Peter, she allowed the truth, the things he'd been trying to make her understand finally saturate her mind. She hadn't been alive at all. She'd been a prisoner.

"She said we'd look for an apartment when she got home," she said, more to herself.

"Azalea, nothing is being done until she returns." Peter seemed to sense her apprehension, her fears starting to rise up.

Pushing the darkness starting to creep into her memories aside, she put on a smile. "Right."

Peter folded his arms across his chest again, giving her the stern look that made her body remotely activate to his every word. This look differed from the one he gave Santos. That look had been full of power and danger. This one, although enough to frighten her when he wanted it to, held the same power, but behind it lurked control and dominance. This man wouldn't hurt her. Wouldn't lock her away from the world.

"What are you doing here, anyway? I thought Daniel was supposed to take you into the city to sign up for a marketing class," he said as though he could hear her thoughts.

"He did." It had been an amazing experience, arguing with Daniel in front of the admissions woman over what address to use for her student application. Daniel had won when he pulled out his phone and threatened to call Peter for his opinion on the subject.

"When does the class start?"

"Next week. I signed up just in time. It's online, too." Which would make her mother more likely to not cancel the class once she returned home.

"No. No online courses. I want you in a classroom, with other people." He shook his head, pulled out his phone, and started typing. "Daniel will take you back this afternoon to get it fixed. I'd take you myself, but I have to meet distributors at Tower, and do the final walk-through at the penthouse. They finished last night."

"I think online is fine. I did almost all of my graphic design work online." Fighting with her mother to keep the class after dealing with the fallback for everything that had happened wouldn't result in a positive outcome.

"I'm sure you do." The corner of his lips twitched.

"Are you making fun of me?" she demanded.

"No. I'm just sure that you'd rather hide online than have to face your mother and tell her you are attending school in person."

"One minute you say I won't want to leave, and I'll stay here, the next you assume you know what I'll do when I go home?" Maybe he'd finally realized her sticking around would cause problems. For both of them, and it would be best for her to go home.

"Have you ever seen baby pictures of yourself?" The complete turnaround on topic caught her off guard. "Have you? Pictures of your mother pregnant with you, or with your father holding you as a baby?"

Her mother didn't have pictures like that, or any, really of her childhood.

"She's not the kind of person to keep photographs." Azalea defended her mother again. Why did she always have to excuse her for the same things Azalea had always felt a bit off?

"Hmmm. There's a huge painting of herself, and pictures of herself in her study, but not of you. That's not strange to you?"

Where the hell was this line of questioning going?

"Do you know something you aren't telling me?" she asked.

"I'm asking questions, that's all. Questions I'm surprised you haven't asked."

Of course, she'd asked them herself. But nothing ever came of it. Her mother refused to discuss her father, and she would find a reason to become irritated if Azalea brought up any topic she didn't want to analyze.

"I'm going upstairs."

"Daniel's waiting for you at the front door," he said firmly.

"He can keep waiting," she threw over her shoulder and stalked out of the room. His footsteps were behind her; she didn't need to look to know it was him.

Well, he could be annoyed, fine. Because she was getting pissed, too. Everyone—everyone seemed to think they knew what was best for her. No one asked—everyone just pushed.

"Azalea." Peter's voice went soft.

She knew what that might mean, but she wasn't in the mood. Not for his heavy-handed ways, not for his overbearing attitude, and certainly not for any damn punishment.

"Do not walk away from me."

"Why? Will you lock me away?" she asked but didn't turn around. She shoved through the door into the main house and stomped through the mudroom toward the living room.

Daniel stood with a smile by the front door. A smile that faded as he caught a glimpse of Peter behind her.

"Uh, Azalea, we going?" he asked with a jerk of his thumb toward the door.

"No."

"Yes." Peter's booming voice overpowered her own.

Azalea grabbed hold of the banister, ready to slingshot around it and run up the stairs, but Peter's pawlike hand landed on her shoulder, stilling her.

Before she could spin around to yell in his face, he had her pressed against the well-polished, intricately carved banister and applied that damn hand of his to her ass.

He didn't even speak while he spanked her! He effortlessly continued to pummel her ass. Right in front of Daniel.

"Peter!" she cried out, trying to block him, but he merely grabbed her hand and pinned it to her back.

"You don't want to face the truth about your mother or your past, that's fine, but you don't raise your voice to me, and you don't walk away from me, and you don't ever tell me no!"

Tears built and fell, but she would not crack. She would not let him think she was going along with his Neanderthal ways.

The slaps finally ceased, and all she could hear was his heavy breathing coupling with her own. He helped her to straighten up, letting go of her hand. She took a step back, wiping her hair from her face then running her hands over her ass. At least he hadn't hiked up her damn skirt.

Daniel wasn't there any longer. It was just the two of them, and they stood glaring at each other. Locked once more in a battle of wills.

"Two more days, Azalea. Until your mother shows up on that doorstep." He jabbed a finger at the front door. "You belong to me for that long at least."

"Belong to you, belong to my mother. Do you think there will ever be a day when I will belong only to myself?"

She ran up the stairs, all the way to his room. Not her room, or their room, his room. Everything belonged to someone else. Nothing was ever truly hers.

By the time she got inside and slammed the door, her lungs burned and tears ran hot down her cheeks. He'd been asking those questions for a reason.

And much like her own mother, he was keeping it all from her.

CHAPTER 18

*P*eter paced the hallway outside his bedroom. How the hell had he let this happen?

He was locked out of his own fucking room!

"Peter!" Daniel jogged the last few steps of the stairs. "I have it." He waved the key. Peter never locked his rooms; there had never been a reason to.

"Thank you." Peter snagged it from him.

"Maybe…don't go in yet," Daniel suggested with some hesitation.

"Why?"

"Because you're still pissed, and she's still pissed, and I've never seen you jump into a spanking like that."

"Are you accusing me of punishing her out of anger?" Peter had already gone over every flitting emotion that occurred before throwing her over that banister. Anger wasn't among them. Fear she wasn't ready for what was coming her way. Irritation she wasn't listening. But not anger. He would never touch her in anger.

"No. I'm saying— Fuck. Man, I've never seen you this

attached to a woman. Like ever." Daniel gestured toward the locked door. "And I've known you since we were kids."

"Get to the point." Because if the point was to make Peter start evaluating his feelings for Azalea, Daniel should start backing away.

"Look, I saw her this morning while we were at the college. She belonged there, man. She just—I don't know, like lit up when we walked past the coffee shop and the bookstore."

"Then why did you let her sign up for an online class?" Peter asked.

"Because." Daniel sighed. "She seemed afraid, and I figured you'd straighten it out. I didn't know you were going to go warlike Dom on her about it, though."

"What the hell does that mean?" Peter gritted his teeth.

"I mean…" Daniel straightened up, like he was coming to her aid. "Did it occur to you to ask her why she wanted the online class? She thinks she's going home with that crazy woman. She thinks she's going to walk out of here and be put right back in that fucking tower her mother kept her in. And if that's not the case, you'll just stash her in your own version." Daniel's voice hardened, and although Peter had heard him use the tone on women in the Annex, on his own submissive, and an asshole or two, he did not appreciate it being turned on him.

Even if he could start to see that it was warranted.

"She said that?" Peter looked at the locked door.

"No. She didn't need to. Maybe if you weren't so hung up on figuring out who her mother is, you'd be able see more of Azalea."

"You got a thing for her?" Peter took a menacing step toward Daniel. Longtime friend or not, if he so much as had a fleeting thought of touching Azalea, Peter would knock it out of his fucking head.

"Of course not." Daniel shook his head. Daniel wasn't into sweet women; he enjoyed the darker side of consent. A woman too willing didn't keep him interested for long. Not that Azalea would be willing with him, but she was too sweet for Daniel. Way too sweet.

"But you're right. You're supposed to be working on getting information on Bellatrix. Not me." Peter gripped the key, letting the teeth bite into his palm. "I'll take Azalea back to school to get her class switched. You—get your ass back to work on figuring out who else Bellatrix works for and how she gets her girls, and where the fuck she's been this whole time."

Daniel clenched his teeth. If he wanted to argue, he managed to bite it back. Without a word, he jogged back down the stairs.

Peter ran a hand over his mouth and down his neck. Daniel hadn't been far off the mark.

Azalea, as far as he knew, hadn't been given many choices in her life. And he hadn't exactly been generous in that department, either. He told himself he was looking after her. Giving her the opportunity to go to class, letting her free to roam the estate. But he wouldn't let her leave. She wasn't free.

She was as trapped with him as she had been growing up.

Peter started to slide the key into the lock, but stopped short of turning it. He'd told her he was going to give her reason to stay. It had to be more than sexual satisfaction that made her go against her mother.

Pulling the key back out, he pocketed it and rapped his knuckles on the door.

"Azalea," he called, rolling his eyes at his own actions. Asking entrance into his own damn room. "Azalea, open up," he ordered, quickly tacking on, "Please."

He heard her walking around. Probably wringing her

hands, trying to decide what to do. He raised his hand to knock again, when the lock unlatched and the door opened.

With a red nose and tearstained cheeks, she greeted him. She'd pulled her hair into a messy bun on top of her head and changed into a pair of yoga pants and an oversized T-shirt. More of Aubree's clothes, no doubt.

Wasting no time, he barged into the room, kicked the door closed, and pulled her to him. She wrapped her arms around his middle and buried her head into his chest.

"I'm sorry," he whispered, tucking her under his chin. "I didn't mean to scare you."

She pulled away from him, wiping her cheeks with her fingers. "You didn't scare me. I was mad."

"You cry when you're mad?" he asked, confused.

"Yes." She nodded, like it was the most natural thing in the world and how come he didn't know that?

"Are you still mad?" he asked cautiously.

"You spanked me. Right in front of Daniel!" She jabbed his chest and walked away from him.

"Daniel walked away as soon as I touched you. He didn't see anything," he assured her, though that couldn't be the problem. Aubree had held her hands while she'd taken a belting only a few days ago.

"He knew. He heard," she said folding her arms over her belly.

"Azalea, when he's with a woman, he spanks her, too. If you think he's judging you—"

"No! Never mind."

She stalked over to the armchair in the corner of the room. Throwing herself into it, she hugged her knees to her chest.

"I can't make this better if you don't tell me. Are you mad at me for spanking you, or because Daniel knows you were spanked?"

She rested her forehead on her knees. For a minute, he thought she wasn't going to say anything, but then she started talking. A bit mumbled given her positioning, so he moved closer to understand her.

"I'm mad because I wasn't mad about it," she muttered.

He rubbed his eyes. If she wasn't going to be rational, how the hell was he going to help her?

"You're mad because you weren't mad. At me?"

"I was mad at you, but then when I got up here—" She let out a low growl. "It's complicated. I wasn't mad at you. I didn't hate it. I mean I didn't like it, but I didn't hate it. You just threw me over the banister and spanked me like some naughty girl."

"Well, you were acting like one," he pointed out.

Her eyes narrowed. "I'm confused and tired and annoyed. You keep pointing out little things about how I was raised, little stuff that maybe I should have picked up. I knew it was strange. I knew my mother was being way overprotective. But I had no choice. I had nowhere to go where she wouldn't find me, and when I tried to leave, she became worse about making me stay."

Peter squatted in front of her, placing his hand on her knee.

"I'm not stupid or as naive as everyone thinks I am," she mumbled. "But she said I'd get my own apartment when she gets back this time, and now—now she'll never let me."

"Azalea, you're an adult. You don't need her protection anymore. She doesn't get to say if you stay with her or not. That's your decision." Peter realized he didn't have the right to make the call for her, either. Even if everything inside him insisted she needed to stay the fuck away from her mother.

"And here?"

"I already told you—it's your call." He stood up and

touched her cheek. "You can't do anything about that right this minute. Wash your face and get changed."

She blinked. "Why?"

"I'm taking you to the school to change your class. Staying with your mom or me or on your own, I think taking marketing will boost your own marketability. You have a talent for graphics, but you put some marketing behind that, and you can really take off."

"What if I don't want to take this class? What if I want to just stick to graphic design and leave it at that?" she asked, obviously testing his new decision to let her have more say.

"If that's what you seriously want, then I won't take you. We'll cancel your registration and be done with it." As much as letting her miss the opportunity would grate on him.

"Okay," she said, pushing off the chair and disappearing into the bathroom. He stared at the closed door.

Okay, she wasn't going, or she was? He sighed. This whole not demanding things of her and letting her walk her own path was going to make his head hurt.

A few minutes later, she reappeared with a clean face, no makeup as he hadn't bothered to get any for her. She was too beautiful to hide behind all that muck of mascara and eyeshadow. She vanished into the closet next. After another minute or two passed, she presented herself in a clean, button-down cotton romper that barely covered her entire ass.

Another of Aubree's damn outfits.

"No, go back in there and change." He wagged a finger at her. No fucking way he was taking her on a college campus with her ass cheeks hanging out the bottom. "It's too fucking cold for something like that anyway," he justified his order.

She laughed. "You lasted an entire five minutes before you started giving orders again."

He relaxed his jaw. "You're testing me?" He took a step toward her. "You're playing games with me?"

Her laugh died, and her smile dropped as he walked her back into the closet. Once she was inside, he grabbed the door handle. "Find something more appropriate. I said I wouldn't force you into anything, but I draw the line at letting anyone put eyes on what's mine."

Before she could protest, he pulled the door closed. He'd wait.

All day if he had to.

CHAPTER 19

Peter tried. He did give it a lot of effort. Azalea could give him that much credit.

But the man didn't give up control easily. He won the wardrobe challenge, not that she had planned on leaving in such a skimpy outfit. Besides the fact the chilly fall wind would cut right through the thin fabric, she had no desire for anyone to see her butt hanging out of the outfit.

Well, anyone other than Peter.

And now that she saw his jealous side—and how much his possessiveness turned her on—she had a new card to play. It probably wasn't very honest to keep goading him until he lost a thread of his control and pulled her up to the bedroom for an afternoon of passion. But, he was a smart man. He knew what she was doing. Thankfully, he never called her out on it. He was too caught up in the moment, which was exactly how she wanted it.

He'd behaved—mostly—while they changed her class from online to on campus, but once back at home, he returned to barking orders.

She dressed in another dress for the evening, since he was

taking her to Tower. She'd taken extra time to wash, dry, and curl her hair. Peter hadn't brought her any makeup, but Aubree had been sweet enough to pick her up the bare essentials. Even her mother had let her wear mascara.

Checking one last time that her earring had the backing in place, she stepped out of the bathroom. Peter had gone to his office to deal with a situation, telling her to go back to his private box once she was finished in the washroom.

One of the security guards followed a few steps behind. Never completely encroaching on her, but near enough for her to be aware of his presence. She sensed this man, unlike Santos, was there solely to protect her, not keep her from running off.

As she neared the box, she noticed two men in staff shirts loitering near the door, holding brooms but not quite using them. She didn't know anyone at Tower, but they didn't look like they belonged. Their shirts were wrinkled, not starchily pressed like the other men she'd seen. And they kept casting glances at her while she walked, and checking behind them.

The guard would intervene if something was wrong, she assured herself when her heart beat faster. The closer she stepped to the entrance, the more the men stared.

She reached for the clasp on the velvet rope separating the area with a shaky hand. Maybe her mother had returned early. Maybe she'd sent men to snatch her back before Peter could interfere.

Looking behind her, she noted the guard was gone. With a panicked breath, she turned to the other two men. They were slowly putting down their brooms. She could run back to Peter's private washroom and could lock herself in. But she didn't have a phone. Would Peter find her?

"Azalea, don't worry," the taller of the two said. She couldn't place his accent. "We aren't here to hurt you."

She took a step back, the heel of her dress catching the

hem of the damn dress Peter had picked out. Stumbling back, she grabbed the back of a chair and righted her footing.

The men moved in on her.

"Who are you?" she demanded. "What do you want?"

"We just want to see you. That's all," the tall one spoke again. The shorter one stayed behind him.

"How do you know who I am?" she asked, still retreating backward.

"Many men know who you are." His sneer sent a cold shiver through her.

"Azalea?" Peter called from down the hall. She turned to face him, relief flooded her at the sight of him hurrying toward her.

He walked past her, and she faced the box to see the men racing down the hall through the VIP boxes and disappear into the stairwell. Peter yanked out his phone and made a call.

"Yes, two of them. Don't let them—what? Fuck." Peter hung up. "Who were they?" he demanded. "Men of your mother's?"

"No. I don't know. I don't think so. I've never seen them before." She closed her eyes momentarily, letting her head settle down.

"Okay. It's okay. They're gone, but I have men looking for them. They couldn't have gotten far." Peter pulled her into his chest and kissed her forehead.

"They said they just wanted to see me, that a lot of men knew who I was. What does that mean?"

"I don't know." He hugged her tighter, to the point air wasn't coming so freely. "Let's get you upstairs."

"Where'd the guard go? He was there and then he was gone."

"I don't know, but I know he's fucking fired." Peter wrapped his arm around her waist and led her to the elevator that would bring them to the penthouse. Now that it was finished, Peter would be moving into it.

She wasn't sure what that would mean for the Annex. He seemed to have a pretty important job taking care of the women there.

"I don't want you walking around alone anymore. In fact, you'll be with me from now on." Once inside the penthouse, Peter locked the door while he gave his instructions.

"What's going on, Peter? You found something out, didn't you?" She followed him into the kitchen where he pulled out two glasses and opened a bottle of wine.

"Let's not get into it right now." He gave her a firm stare. He knew something, all right, but he wasn't divulging it.

"You said I'd be making my own choices. How can I do that when you hold things back?"

He put the wine bottle down and captured her face between his palms.

"I don't know anything for certain. I have people looking into it, and once I know for sure, I'll tell you everything."

"You swear it?"

"On my mother and father's grave," he vowed.

"Okay," she whispered. "As soon as you know."

He nodded, dropping a kiss to her lips before going back to pouring the wine. "Did they say anything else?"

"No, you came up before they could." She took the glass of red wine he offered her.

Peter leaned forward on the counter, pressing his hands flat onto the countertop. His mind seemed to be working in overdrive. The silence unsettled her.

"You think my mother's involved," she said gently. Not accusing him. How could she? At this point, she was fairly certain the things she didn't know about her mother greatly outweighed those she did. And how could she trust someone she knew so little about?

"I think she's involved. I don't know how deeply. She's worked with my uncle in the past, and other heads of family who dealt with—" He brought his gaze to hers. "Things a daughter shouldn't know, until it's confirmed."

"Because once I know —or suspect—it will change my view of my mother?" She put the glass of wine down. She didn't need the subtlety of the wine, she needed something much harder.

"My mother worked in the Annex." Peter turned around and leaned back. His hands fisted on the edge of the countertop, his eyes focused intently on her.

"I didn't know that." She didn't know anything about his family. Too caught up in her own drama, she'd never bothered to find out.

"My uncle, Samuel Titon, bought her at an auction in Naples. Her own father had sold her to the American asshole for a tidy profit."

Azalea hid her horrified reaction and remained silent. He seemed to need to get this out, and she wouldn't stop him. Not when he opened up to her.

"She worked in the Annex. My uncle whored her out to his friends, and anyone with deep-enough pockets to fork over his price. She had no choice, nowhere to go. Hell, she barely understood English for the first few years. My father was away at school, getting his degree."

Peter shifted his feet. "See, since he was the second son, he stood to inherit nothing. That's how the Titon family works. So, he went and got a degree—figuring he'd help the family business with his financial expertise. He met my mother when he came home."

Azalea eased closer to him, her hand inches away from his fist.

"My uncle sold my mother to my father. He made a nice profit, and it took my father nearly five years of working for

Samuel before he paid him off."

"Your father bought your mother?" She couldn't understand these workings. Why would anyone think they could buy or sell another person?

"He did. And he gave her the option to leave, the moment she was released from the Annex. My father had been seeing her—well, as much as he could, given their roles in the house. Instead of taking her freedom and leaving, she married him, and although she despised my uncle, she remained. She stopped working in the Annex, though."

"If your father was half as possessive as you are, I don't think she could have even if she wanted to." Azalea slid her hand on top of his, feeling and needing the connection their touch gave her.

The corner of his lip kicked up in something that resembled a smile.

"When I was a kid, I thought my uncle was perfect. He had so much power. Grown men bent to his will. He was so fucking god-like. I didn't understand my mother's feelings toward him. She never outright disrespected him, but she always seemed so unhappy when he was around. Ash didn't know much about his father, either. He spent most of his time with his mother. But when I learned what actually went on in the Annex, and how my parents met…" His jaw clenched.

"It wasn't something I could un-know. The great man I thought my uncle was crumbled like a five-day-old cookie, and I couldn't put the pieces back together again. I didn't understand why my father would keep working for him, or why my mother didn't want me to quit, either. By then I was already running collections with my dad."

"You didn't have many choices growing up, either." Azalea stepped in front of him, resting her hands on his hips. "I get it. You don't want me to know anything I can't un-know unless it's completely necessary. You're still trying to protect me, even though in a few days, I could be gone. I could be back with my mother, in my own bed."

She noticed the tic in his jaw. "No, you can't tell me I still can't talk about it. The time is coming."

"I don't feel right about her. From what I've been finding out—there's something wrong here." He framed her face, his thumbs running along her jaw.

"And like my mother, you want to protect me from everything. But you can't." She moved up to her toes, pressing her lips against his. "I always seem to wiggle out anyway." She grinned against his mouth.

His hands moved from her face and cupped her ass, clutching her flesh hard. "That's not exactly an endearing quality, Azalea. Staying put is being obedient, and your obedience makes my cock hard."

Peter pulled her against him, letting her feel the hard length of his cock pressing against his slacks.

Everything in the world was topsy-turvy at the moment. She didn't truly know her mother, and she barely knew Peter. But she'd never once felt as safe in her own home as she did when Peter looked at her.

He'd never let anything happen to her. And whatever that meant, in whatever form his protection came—love or responsibility—she craved it.

Sliding her hands down his chest, she reached for his belt buckle, quickly undoing it while she stared into his eyes. The cocky smile she'd seen too many times to count appeared.

"What are you doing?" he asked.

"Whatever I want. Feel free to punish me later." She winked and yanked down his zipper. She felt his cock, hot and unyielding, against her fingers. Wrapping them around his length, she drew it out of his pants and kept her eyes on his while she sank to the floor.

"Azalea," he protested, but she pushed his protest away.

"Add that to my list of bad deeds." Once she was on her knees, his cock level with her mouth, she flicked her tongue over the head. Testing the taste and texture—immediately wanting more of both.

"No." His hand wound into her hair, pulling her back painfully until she was looking back up at him. "You don't just take, pretty girl. You beg." The control, the raw power of him shone down at her. She'd tried to snatch the power for a fleeting second, to give him what she thought he needed. But what he needed, what made him whole, was being the one holding her hair. Being the strength that kept the power ebbing and flowing between them. She'd get to suck his cock, but it would be on his terms.

And it struck her, staring up at him with a shocked smile paused on her lips, her body melted in his hands when he took the reins.

"Peter." She swallowed.

He chuckled, that low *tsk tsk* sort of laugh he had. "That's not how a pretty girl begs." He tapped her cheek. Replacing her hand with his own, he fisted his shaft and brought the head of his cock right to her lips. "Beg me to fuck your face."

Oh fuck. Yes, that sounded much better than what she had planned.

"Peter, please, use me—fuck my mouth." What she thought would humiliate—empowered. She parted her lips and slid her tongue out, willing him to do what he wanted. Because she was his to do as he wished.

"Oh, pretty girl." He pushed forward, the silky-smooth head ran over her tongue, and, when it hit the back of her throat, she did her best to swallow. When she sputtered, he retreated a bit, but only for a split second before driving right back into her.

She hummed as he gripped her head and thrust into her

mouth. He growled, and she made a silent note to thank Aubree for the tip.

The harder he fucked her throat, the easier it became to give over to his power.

"Fuck." He yanked free, jerking her head back again to look down at her. A string of saliva kept her lips and his cock connected. "I need to be inside you." He gave a curt nod and reached down. Hooking her under her arms, he hauled her to her feet.

"Peter. Oh."

He yanked her head to the side, sinking his teeth into her neck and making her all the more pliable.

He cupped her ass, picked her up, and put her on the counter. "You'd better not be wearing any fucking panties." He was back to using that angry rumble, the one that made her pussy slick for him.

"You never gave me any," she answered. Asking Aubree for pants or to grab some mascara from the store was one thing, asking for panties was something entirely different.

"And I never will." His vow held the weight of promised time, time she wasn't sure they would have.

He pulled down on her neckline and groaned when it wouldn't budge. "This fucking thing." With two hands he shredded it from her chest. Finally bare to him, he captured one nipple in his mouth. Sucking hard and licking the already-peaked nub, he was a man starved.

"Peter!" She grabbed his shoulders when he yanked the skirt and pulled her to the edge of the counter.

"Hold on, pretty girl." He slid her off the counter and impaled her with one quick thrust. In the space of a breath, she was filled with his thick length. Every inch of it. Filling and stretching. Her mind reeled.

He thrust upward, into her while holding her. "Fuck. Fuck," he chanted.

"Oh god," she cried out, kissing his neck, biting down on his ear.

"Not yet. Don't you fucking unravel yet," he demanded, walking them to the wall and pressing her against it.

He let her lower one foot to the floor but held the other thigh up, hooked around his now-naked hip. Cupping her chin with a free hand, he drew her gaze to his.

"Now, come. Fucking explode on my cock," he demanded, thrusting into her, grinding against her clit. Just the tone of his voice had her at the edge.

"Oh—fuck, yes, fuck—"

His dark eyes locked with hers. Her back rubbed against the wall with each push of his cock into her, filling her so sweetly. He fucked her harder, giving her a bite with his thrust, spiraling her mind.

"Now, Azalea, now, pretty girl." He moved his hand from her jaw to her throat. Pinning her there, just enough pressure for her to feel him, to know the power he held. Too much of a squeeze and it would be bad, but the right amount—like he applied—stole her breath—focused her mind on the hard fucking he was giving her.

She couldn't get enough air to speak.

"There's my girl—you like this—oh fuck." He slipped in his own control, but quickly brought his attention back to her. "Be my good girl, my pretty girl. Come for me, Azalea, come hard.

His fingers pressed into her throat a hair more, and it was all her body needed. He eased up as she screamed out with the waves coursing through her body. A heated tingling ran over her skin and her mind blanked. The only cognitive thought being focused on the hard pounding of her orgasm shattering her.

"Fuck. Fuck. Fuck." He released the pressure, but kept his

hand on her throat while he thrust up at her—finding his own release.

Another hard push and then he stilled, his hot breath running over her face, his forehead pressed against her, and his fingers lightly petting her throat.

"Pretty girl," he whispered. "Such a good girl."

Slowly, he put her back on both feet, his cock sliding out and soiling her dress in the process. She couldn't care less. His cum seeping out of her, dripping on her thigh, only cemented his ownership.

"Let me see." He cupped her chin and pushed it up, examining her throat.

"I'm fine, Peter. You wouldn't hurt me." She wrapped her hand around his wrist.

His gaze fluttered to hers. "No, I wouldn't. But I want to make sure you aren't bruised. Your skin is too fucking fair." Seeming satisfied he hadn't marked her, he pulled up his pants, zipping and buttoning, but leaving the belt hanging open at his waist. His untucked shirt gave him a disheveled look she wasn't used to seeing on him.

"You did ruin the dress, though." She toyed with the frayed edges of the bodice.

He cast her a quick glance. "We'll stay here tonight." He snagged the glass of wine from the counter and downed it in two gulps. After pressing a quick kiss to her lips, he headed out of the kitchen.

She held the dress together in her fist, staring at the empty room.

Had she done something wrong?

CHAPTER 20

Peter pulled his car through the gates toward the garage. He wouldn't be leaving the estate until Azalea's mother had been dealt with.

Azalea sat beside him, hands locked between her knees. Thankfully, he'd had some clothing sent over to his penthouse, otherwise she'd be wearing that torn dress.

After telling her about his mother, how his parents became a couple, he'd felt splayed open. On display. And she'd been perfect.

She'd touched him, softly drew him back to the present. When she'd sunk to her knees before him and pulled out his cock, something clicked into place. She was exactly where she wanted to be, and right where he needed her.

With a simple touch, she could soothe him. It hadn't taken much more than that to draw out the darkness from within him. The need to devour and conquer. And he'd done both.

He had checked her for bruising on her neck again before leaving the penthouse. None. He'd been careful, but she was so fucking fair, so gentle—he had needed to be sure.

His promise to let her decide, to let her walk right out of

his life if she chose to, kept screeching through his mind. Reminding him what a fool's promise it had been.

Never had he gone back on a promise. But how the fuck would he honor this one?

Azalea opened her door and got out the moment he pushed the gear into park. He hadn't spoken much to her that morning, mostly because he didn't trust what he'd say. She'd touched a nerve, had soothed it, and now he didn't know how to act. He didn't deserve to possess such purity, such innocence, yet there she was, waiting for him to claim her.

He joined her at the garage door, linking his fingers with hers. She paused for a beat then relaxed in his grip.

With a nod, he opened the door and waved her inside.

"Peter! Fuck. Thank god, you're back!" Daniel ran down the hall toward them.

"What's wrong?" Peter asked, pulling Azalea along behind him.

"Bellatrix is in Ash's office," Daniel said, a little out of breath either from panic or the job.

"My mother? She's here?" Azalea pitched forward.

"Yes."

"Okay. That's fine." Peter nodded again, tightening his hold on Azalea. "We'll be right there. Is she alone?"

Daniel shook his head. "No, that's just it. She's not. She has four assholes with her, and two more outside in her car. Didn't you see it when you drove up?"

Peter had been too preoccupied in his own fucking head to notice. He'd driven straight to the garage and not paid any attention to the front of the house.

"Peter, maybe I should talk with her alone?" Azalea's soft voice penetrated the tension in the hall.

"No. Absolutely not." Peter pointed at Daniel. "Did you get the information I wanted?"

Daniel looked at Azalea then back to Peter. "Yeah. You were right. Around the same time."

Fuck. Peter took a deep breath.

"What? What's going on?" Azalea pulled free of Peter's grip.

"Azalea…" How to tell her? He needed more time, more information to show her.

"I don't think Bellatrix is your real mother." Peter turned around to face her.

Her eyes widened, and her mouth opened. "What? Why?"

"Well, you don't look anything like her," Daniel offered.

Peter would kick him later for that.

"So? She told me I took after my father," Azalea quickly stated. "Look, whatever it is, we'll ask her." She touched Peter's chest. "I'm not going anywhere today." A promise. A vow.

After a long moment of hesitation, Peter nodded and led her to Ash's office. Daniel followed, and Johnny was already stationed outside the office.

Peter pushed the office door open, and they both filed inside.

Bellatrix, though carrying a few more wrinkles than the pictures in her house showed, didn't seem to have aged. Her dark, wavy hair hung loose around her face. Makeup perfectly applied.

"Oh! Azalea!" Bellatrix flung her arms open but didn't step toward her daughter.

"Mother." Azalea waited a beat then walked into her mother's arms.

"I was so worried!" Bellatrix looked over Azalea's shoulder at Peter, her eyes narrowing.

"I'm fine. I'm good," Azalea said, pulling back. When she tried to move away, Bellatrix grabbed her hand, holding it the way a mother might hold a child's hand to cross the road. But the grip was tighter. Had more purpose.

"When Santos finally told me what was going on, I came right home."

"Everything is okay," Azalea said again, looking back at Peter.

"Santos told me you took her, that you found her locked up in her room and took her. I should thank you. Santos shouldn't have locked her door. He—acted poorly." Bellatrix focused her attention on Peter.

The other men in the room stood along the wall with their hands folded in front of them. Trained monkeys waiting for the witch to give them leave to fly.

"I have some questions for you." Peter ignored the stare of the men and walked around Ash's desk.

"I have a few for you myself." Bellatrix gave a forced giggle.

"Mine first," Peter said coolly. He wasn't buying the motherly act. It was poorly executed, but Azalea seemed comfortable with it. Probably because she'd never known true motherly affection or care.

"Who is Azalea's father?" he asked, not sitting down in his chair, but pressing his fingertips into the desk.

"That's an awfully personal question to ask. It's quite personal, and frankly none of your business." Bellatrix's lip twitched.

"Does Azalea know him?"

"You're quite nosy," Bellatrix said.

"And you're awfully secretive."

"My secrets are mine," Bellatrix said in a low tone. "Azalea, we're going home, now."

"Mother—"

"Enough." Bellatrix snapped her attention to her daughter. "I understand you didn't have a choice in coming here—"

She turned her glare to Peter. "You were forced. But you will return home with me now."

"She's well past the age of consent. She will do what she wants, not what you tell her to do." Peter stepped to the side of the desk, ready to move in if Bellatrix threatened Azalea in any way.

"She is coming home with me, and you can kiss my boots for not calling the police and reporting the kidnapping!" A gleam of raw rage simmered in her otherwise-controlled demeanor.

"What sort of business do you do with the Jansen family? Are you providing him with girls? Maybe young girls ripped from their families and sold to women like you?" Peter took another step, keeping his focus on Azalea ,but noticing the men starting to tense near the door. Daniel and Johnny were just outside, they'd be at his side in seconds if anything went wrong.

"Mother?" Azalea turned a confused look to Bellatrix. "What's he talking about?"

"He's a liar, Azalea. I told you. Men will say anything to get you to do what they want, and this man wants you. He'll say anything to make me look like a villain."

"You kept your daughter locked away!" Peter pointed out. "It doesn't take much work to expose that."

"I kept her safe." Bellatrix jerked a nod. "And I still need to, apparently. We're leaving, and if you so much as take a breath near my daughter again, you'll see the consequences."

Azalea tried to break free.

"Wait."

"No. We're leaving." Bellatrix tightened her hold and gave a nod to her men. All four moved in, surrounding them. Johnny and Daniel rushed into the room, but her men already had their guns drawn.

"No. Daniel, no!" Azalea cried out when he pulled his gun.

"It's okay. It's fine." She turned her head, her eyes full of fear and uncertainty. "I'll be okay. I'll go home. Peter, you can come see me, or I'll come here," she said with a plea in her voice.

She'd go with Bellatrix to avoid bloodshed, but she wasn't choosing her mother.

"You don't have to go with her," Peter said, reaching for her.

"I do. It's okay. It's fine." Her voice cracked. She wasn't fine.

Peter's jaw tensed. Letting her go wasn't an option.

Four men.

"Oh, for hell's sake!" Bellatrix, apparently tired of the discussion, grabbed a gun from one of her men and pointed it at Johnny. Aiming low, she pulled the trigger, taking out his kneecap and making him crumble to the floor.

Chaos erupted. Johnny's screams, Azalea's cry, Daniel's demand for her to drop the fucking gun. Everything became background noise when Bellatrix took the gun and pressed the barrel to her daughter's head.

"We are leaving. I've had enough of this silliness."

"Mother?" Azalea froze, her eyes frantically searching the room.

Her men moved in closer. Daniel continued to train his gun on her, but with the huddle, he wouldn't be able to get a clean shot.

Peter felt for his own gun and found nothing. He'd left it upstairs. Fuck!

Helpless, he watched as Azalea was spirited away, out of the office. He walked stoically down the hall, hearing another cry from Azalea when the huddled group met up with more of his men.

"Stand down," Peter called, waving his hands. "Let her go."

If they disagreed—and Peter was pretty damn sure they did—they kept it to themselves.

He'd find a way to get her back. He wouldn't let her just disappear.

"Let's go." Bellatrix swept Azalea out the front door, the gun still pointed at her but no longer butted up against her. Two others jumped from one of the two cars parked in front. After ushering the two women into the back seat of one, they all jumped in and sped off.

"Lock the gate!" Daniel called, but there wasn't a man positioned at the gate.

"Let her go. I'm not going to chance Azalea's safety," Peter said in a hard voice. His heart wouldn't stop racing, and his mind kept focusing on Azalea's fear. Replaying the utter shock on Azalea's face when her mother pressed the pistol against her head.

"Safety!? Her mother just put a fucking gun to her head and took her!" Daniel bellowed.

Peter turned a cool eye on him. "Go take care of Johnny. Then I want every bit of fucking information you can get me on that fucking Gothel bitch." Peter pointed at his men standing at the door. "No one leaves. We are going back to get her. She is not to spend one fucking night in that witch's house! Not one fucking night!" Peter made his way up the stairs to his room.

He needed his fucking gun.

He needed to start making plans.

He needed to get a fucking grip and remind himself he would get her back. He would.

She belonged to him.

She belonged with him.

CHAPTER 21

Something died nearby. The rancid smell of rot consumed the small room where Azalea had been stashed. Not quite a cell—there were painted walls, clean sheets on the bed, but nothing like the comforts of her old suite at home.

Because her mother hadn't taken her home.

After she'd pulled her away from the safety of Peter's presence, she'd shoved her into the back of her mother's Cadillac and driven several hours outside of the city limits. She had tried to ask where they were headed, but her mother had simply ignored her.

For two days, she had been alone in her current room. A small attached bathroom had enough room for a toilet and a stand-up shower. The floor was cold beneath her bare feet; the thin tiles long ago had lost any texture or coloring, leaving behind a dull, egg-colored floor. At least she'd been given a blanket and a pillow for the bed.

Her mother hadn't bothered to explain anything. Hadn't said a word after marching her from Peter's life. And, now, she'd stashed her in this room. For what? To live out the remainder of her life in solitary confinement?

Was this a punishment? Or was something worse coming her way?

She could try to bang on the door again, call for someone —but, so far, her cries had gone unheeded. She knew someone was out there, on the other side, because every so often she heard footsteps.

The confinement reminded her of the first time she found herself locked in her suite. She'd cried for hours before calming down. Her mother had explained it was for her safety. She had been having a party and wanted to be sure Azalea was kept safe.

Fear had welled up in Azalea's seven-year-old chest. Tears ran down her face, and when the darkness of night came, she crawled under the blankets and cried herself to sleep.

Only this time, Azalea was well past seven, and she knew the darkness wasn't going to signal bedtime. This time, it would signal something much more sinister.

If only she had pressed Peter for more information about his suspicions about her mother.

I don't think your mother is your real mother he'd said. How could that be? She didn't remember there being anyone else in her life. Not even her father. There hadn't been anyone.

The doorknob jiggled, startling her. Azalea stood, folding her hands in front of her, expecting her mother to breeze in as she always did after a stint of putting Azalea under lock and key.

"Get cleaned up. You're expected upstairs in half an hour." A man—one Azalea had never met before—with a large scar covering his left cheek, and beady black eyes threw a bundle of clothes on the narrow bed.

"My mother wants to see me?" she asked, attempting to keep the hope from reaching her voice.

The man sneered. "Bellatrix requires your attendance. Don't dawdle. I'll be back for you." And with that, he slammed the door shut again, and locked it.

Azalea looked through the clothing, a soft linen dress, crumpled by his manhandling, and undergarments. If she went with wrinkles, her mother would be agitated.

Finding two small nails jutting out of the drywall, she pulled on them to make a hook and hung the dress. The steam from the shower should help get some of the wrinkles out.

She made quick work of washing her hair. The smell of the dank room had to have seeped into the strands. There was no hair dryer or curling iron, so she did the best she could with the thin towels she'd been given and her fingers as a comb.

Although she had no way of telling the time, when the lock unlatched again, she had no doubt the man had arrived at his promised time.

She stood in the center of the room, the dress mostly wrinkle-free, and her hair loose around her shoulders. He gave her a once-over, grunted, and motioned for her to follow him.

It had been dark when she'd been dragged into the small room, and she hadn't been able to see her surroundings. But now that it was light, and she wasn't being forced to move, she took in the dungeon-like appearance. Rooms lined the hallway on both sides. No windows on any of the doors, only large bolts.

She paused when she heard a whimper coming from behind one of the doors.

"Let's go." The man with his large hands reached back and pulled her forward again.

Who was that? Did her mother have girls down there?

Azalea stumbled but quickly found her footing and

climbed the stairwell. Bright beams of light blinded her as she stepped onto the landing.

Shielding her eyes with her cupped hand, she blinked several times before she adjusted to the lighting.

"Azalea." Her mother's cold voice drew her attention. "Put your hand down. You look like a fool." Her hand was smacked away.

Blinking away the last of the fog, Azalea focused on her mother. The epitome of perfection, as always. Not a single hair out of place, her makeup applied carefully, and her back straight as a damn broomstick. How is it Azalea hadn't noticed until then how much her mother resembled the witches depicted in all the fairy tales she'd been told growing up?

"You showered. Good. We will have to do something with your hair, though. It needs to be blown dry and curled, I think. Yes, big wavy curls. And you need a bit of mascara to highlight those damn eyes of yours, and a touch of blush to showcase your cheekbones."

Azalea jerked her face away when her mother pinched her cheeks.

"Why? And, where are we?" Azalea surveyed the room. Not unlike her mother's office at home, the room was littered with self-portraits.

"We're in my home," her mother said with a tinge of relief, as though a weight were being lifted from her.

"But—"

"Oh, you know nothing, you stupid child," Bellatrix snapped. "I am going to be so relieved when this is finished."

"When what is finished? You're talking in riddles!" Azalea had never raised her voice to her mother, until that moment. Enough already. She couldn't take any more. Her body ached, her head throbbed, and she had no idea where the hell she was.

Bellatrix's eyes widened at Azalea's outburst. Taking steady steps toward her, she kept her hard gaze on Azalea.

Azalea's head snapped from the impact of her mother's hand landing fiercely against her cheek.

"You will mind your tongue," Bellatrix seethed. Taking a step back, she smoothed her hands over her flat stomach, taking a deep breath.

Azalea's cheek pulsated with pain, but she ignored it. Not wanting to give satisfaction to her mother—her obviously deranged mother.

"What happened to you?" Azalea asked, trying to grasp onto something—anything that would explain her mother's sudden turn in behavior toward her. "Are you sick?"

Bellatrix laughed, a deep, sinister laugh Azalea could not recall hearing before.

The door to the room opened, and two men walked in, Santos hung limply between them. He raised his head, one eye swollen shut. His bottom lip was puffy and bleeding. Azalea doubted he'd be able to speak if he wanted to.

"Mother," Azalea spoke softly. "I don't understand. Why —" She stopped and took a shaky breath. "Why are we here? What's happening?"

"Azalea, it's time for you to take a husband," her mother said with a sneer.

"Take a husband?" What the hell was happening? Her mother had always been too protective. Why would she even consider having her marrying anyone?

"Yes. Well, I'm not sure the man who buys you will actually make you his wife, or treat you with any sort of husbandly affection, but that doesn't really matter."

Azalea's breath caught in her throat.

"Your little stunt the past few weeks almost ruined the whole thing, but luckily I came home in time to fix it." Bellatrix walked around her, appraising her with her stare. "Did

Peter, the meddling ass, did he take your virginity?" she asked, coming toe-to-toe with Azalea.

"I—" There was no good way to answer that question. If she lied, her mother would know, and if she told the truth, her mother would be angry. "I need you to slow down. What's going on? What do you mean 'buy me'?"

Bellatrix let out a huff of air. "He did. Those damn Titon men. Just take whatever they want. Though I doubt you gave him much trouble." She raised a dark eyebrow at Azalea. "That's okay. As long as that pussy of yours is good and tight, you'll still fetch a good price."

She walked away from Azalea, circling around the desk and opening a drawer.

"You're going to sell me?" Azalea said the words, but her brain still would not comprehend them.

Bellatrix sighed again, pulling a revolver from the desk drawer. "You're too old to keep locked away. It's your twenty-third birthday. Did you forget your own birthday?"

Her birthday. Azalea blinked. She had forgotten—not that she had any clue what day it actually was. Days without seeing the sunlight would do that.

"Why would you keep me locked away? I don't understand! You were always so protective of me, and now you want to sell me to some—some—"

"Azalea, please pay attention," her mother snapped. "I have no use for you any longer. That's the truth of it. And keeping you is more of a hassle than it's worth. I could kill you—" She waved the barrel of the revolver in Azalea's general direction. "But look at you! That hair, those damn eyes of yours, and your body was made for a man's pleasure. You do have some worth left. What better birthday present than a new life."

Azalea rubbed her eyes. Why couldn't she get her mind to clear enough to understand what was being said?

"Don't worry about that dizziness you're feeling," her mother said. "Just a side-effect of the sedative. Once we're done here, you can go back down to your cell and sleep."

"Done?" Azalea blinked a few more times. How had she slipped her a sedative? She hadn't eaten or drunk. She'd only taken a shower, and brushed her teeth.

The toothpaste? Could it have been drugged?

"Yes. After you've rested some more, you'll be brought up here to get ready. There are several prospective buyers coming tonight for dinner. You'll be showcased then."

"Prospective…" Azalea's eyelids were too heavy to keep open. She leaned against the armchair.

"Yes, and I'm sure you won't disappoint me. You'll smile, and you'll speak when spoken to, and I'll make a tidy profit." Bellatrix lifted her gun. "I truly don't like to be disappointed." Swinging her arm to the right, she pulled the trigger.

Azalea's ears rang from the sound of the gunshot, but what stole her attention was Santos falling to the ground in a heap. The bullet had struck him in the center of his forehead. Blood pooled on the floor. The men who had been holding him flanked Azalea and grabbed her arms.

Was she next? Would her mother end her life just as it was about to begin?

Did Peter even know where she was?

Peter took over her thoughts while her mind slowed to a crawl then a stop, and the darkness she'd been chasing took over completely.

CHAPTER 22

Peter slammed the door to the office and stalked to the wet bar his cousin kept. A stiff drink would not be enough to wipe away the anger and fear and guilt lingering over him, but it would at least dull it enough to let him think more clearly.

Where the fuck would Bellatrix have taken Azalea? They'd already searched the townhouse and the small office building registered in Bellatrix's name. Nothing. Not a fucking trace.

"Peter." Daniel barged into the room.

"What?" Peter downed another gulp of whiskey.

"Hunter and Damien have arrived."

Peter poured another finger of liquor. "Send them in. What are you waiting for?"

Daniel opened his mouth like he was about to speak, but shook his head and disappeared again.

Hunter and Damien walked in, wearing confused, but irritated expressions.

"Peter." Hunter extended his hand, but Peter didn't bother with the pleasantries.

"Damien, sit." Damien worked for Hunter, which was the only reason he was involved at all. They needed Hunter's uncle to cooperate.

"Peter, what's going on?" Hunter demanded.

Peter sighed. "Azalea's gone." He breathed out, the pain at the memory of her being spirited away hadn't dulled a fraction even with the copious amount of whiskey he'd drunk.

"Azalea? The girl my uncle was asking about?" Hunter pressed.

"Yes. Her name is Azalea Gothel. Except"—Peter looked at Damien—"I don't think that's her real name."

"Okay, so what does that have to with me, or Damien?"

Peter kept his focus on Damien. "Are you an only child?" Peter asked.

Damien laughed. "What does that have to do with anything?"

"Are you?" Peter pressed. He needed to be absolutely sure before he dropped it in Damien's lap.

"Yes—well—no." Damien's smile waned. "I had a younger sister, but she was killed. A long time ago, when I was a kid."

"Killed? Or taken?" Peter pressed, knowing the look of discomfort in Damien's eyes too well.

"Taken. Kidnapped when she was barely a year old. But we assumed—I assumed." Damien shoved his hands in his front pockets. "Why are you asking all this?"

"And did Bellatrix do business with anyone in your family?"

"I was a kid. I don't know." Damien shrugged, looking more agitated.

"If she works with my uncle now, she more than likely dealt with Damien's father at some point. He worked alongside my uncle when we were kids."

Loyalty didn't die off when a member of the family died, no matter how loose the relation.

"Are you trying to tell me Bellatrix kidnapped my sister?" Damien stepped forward, his voice hard and full of threat. "You'd better have some real evidence to suggest something like that."

Peter picked up a picture from his desk and handed it to him. "That's a still photo from the security camera at Tower. If she's not related to you, then it's one hell of a coincidence."

Hunter moved closer to Damien to look at the shot. He let out a low whistle. "Hell, that hair."

"Yeah, like gold spun with streaks of silver, just like your man here. And the eyes, and the nose— Hell. She could be his fucking twin."

"Why didn't you say something when we were here?" Damien asked, still staring at the photograph.

"I didn't recognize it until you were leaving. I wasn't sure. And I didn't want to say anything until I knew for certain. But then Bellatrix showed up." Peter dragged his hand through his hair.

What a fucking shit show that meeting had been.

"But you're sure, now?"

"We're sure Bellatrix isn't her mother." Daniel walked into the room. "It looks like Bellatrix was once a girl in the Annex."

Peter's brows came together. He hadn't known that.

"She was in the Annex but had been bought. After that, there's no record of her until she showed up as a vendor. We couldn't find record of her at first because when she was here, she went by Bella Schmale. Not much of a name. She must have changed it when she was bought."

"Who bought her?" Peter demanded.

"Kevin Simon." Daniel glanced at Damien.

"My father?" Damien nearly roared the question. Hunter put his hand on Damien's shoulder.

"From what the ledgers show—and it took some deciphering of Samuel's code, but yeah, Kevin Simon bought her. After the sale, there's nothing. Samuel wouldn't have record of what happened to the women after they left the Annex."

"Do you remember there being a nanny, maybe?" Hunter asked Damien.

"No. There was never another woman in our fucking house. My father stayed loyal to my mother. To his very last breath." Damien's eyes darkened, his hands fisted.

"Somehow Bellatrix had access to Azalea. And she has her again. We need to find out where she took her." Peter focused on Hunter. "Your uncle might know. I need a meeting with him, I need to know where she keeps her girls."

Hunter shook his head. "He's not going to give up that information. Not to a Titon. You're out of the business, remember? And letting that information out would damage his own business."

"She has Azalea." Peter ground the sentence out. He was fucking sick of the games played by the families. All the formalities and bullshit. If one fucking hair was bent out of shape on Azalea's head when he found her, every one of the fuckers would pay.

"I'll get the information you need." Hunter pulled out his phone.

"I'm going with you when you find her," Damien said, sitting down in the chair and pressing his hands into his knees.

Peter nodded. He would need good men to go with him. It was doubtful Bellatrix would welcome them with open arms.

Hunter stepped out of the room with his phone pressed against his ear.

"Did you find anything else in my uncle's ledgers?" Peter asked Daniel.

"Nothing that made sense or was worth anything. He

dealt with Bellatrix later, buying girls from her every once in a while. Mostly, he sold to her."

"If she hurts Azalea—"

"She won't." Hunter stepped inside the room again. "She can't hurt her."

"Why?" Damien asked.

"Because she's selling her. There's an auction for her tonight."

CHAPTER 23

With a less groggy head but still confused mind, Azalea was led up to a dressing room. She didn't know how long she'd slept. She only knew she was being primped in order to be pimped.

"Only a little makeup. Her innocence is where her beauty lies." Her mother floated into the cramped room. The woman holding the curling iron in one hand and a large amount of Azalea's hair in the other nodded.

"Of course, madame," she said. "Any coloring on her lips? They are full. Men will like to see them."

Bellatrix tapped her chin while inspecting Azalea, making her feel more like a prized ham than her daughter. "Yes. I think you're right. They will definitely like them."

"Mother." Azalea tried again to reason with her. "I'm sorry I wasn't able to get away from Peter. I'm sorry I wasn't home when you got back, but you can't just—you won't, will you? Sell me?"

Bellatrix's cold stare sent shivers through Azalea.

"Azalea, you aren't my daughter. Not by blood. Not by anything. You were revenge, and now that you've served that purpose, it's time for you to go away." It was her mother's voice. Soft and purposeful like usual, but the words—so callous—so cold.

"I'm not your daughter?" Peter had warned her, had told her, but she had rejected the idea.

"I took you—from a man who thought he could discard me so easily. He loved his wife, and cast me aside—but it was also because of you. It was you he loved so much. And you made that silver-haired witch so damn happy when you were born. When he cast me out, I bided my time, but then I came for you."

"You kidnapped me?" Azalea's disbelief put her into action, and she started to rise from the chair. With a quick shove, the hairdresser pushed her back.

"Stay down, or I'll strap you there," the woman threatened, shaking the hot iron at her.

"I needed you to stay hidden, away from prying eyes. I went into business on my own and have made quite a success of it. You'll be my biggest profit this quarter, though. Which is fitting, given how much money you've cost me over the years."

Azalea's heart clenched. She'd been kidnapped. And, now, she was being sold. To who? What man would buy another human being?

Not a kind one, of that she was sure.

"Ah, there we go. She's finally understanding." Bellatrix patted her cheek.

Azalea slapped her hand away and glared up at her.

"I will not be sold." Peter would get there. He wouldn't allow this to happen. He'd been trying to warn her about her mother. He knew—in how much detail, she wasn't sure, but he knew Bellatrix was bad news. He wouldn't let this happen. No one was buying her tonight.

"You raise your voice and then your hand to me?" Bellatrix's eyes narrowed, her lips thinned, and her nostrils flared.

"If you mark me, your clients will be displeased," Azalea snapped at her, recognizing the fight in her mother's eyes. She'd seen it before when she'd snuck down and witnessed her dealing with her men.

"Move." Bellatrix pushed the hairdresser away from her and snagged a pair of shears from the table. "You're right. They won't like if you have bruises on your delicate skin. But they won't care about your hair like you do." She gathered it in one hand, and no matter how much Azalea struggled and tried to smack her away, she was no match for Bellatrix.

Azalea could feel each strand being pulled away as Bellatrix cut through the mass of hair. The weight eased, and by the time Bellatrix tossed the scissors back on the table, the ends of Azalea's hair barely reached her shoulders.

It had been chopped off.

Tears flooded her eyes. She touched the ends, the raw, jagged ends. All of it—gone.

"Clean up that mess and go with short curls," Bellatrix ordered. "If she gives you any more trouble, strap her down and gag her. We can present her that way if she chooses. Though I'm sure any man who finds her bound and gagged attractive will probably not be kind and gentle with her once he has her."

Azalea didn't look up at her. She didn't need to. The chill in her voice was clear enough.

"You're lucky." The hairdresser ran a comb through her short locks.

"How is that?" Azalea asked, feeling as pathetic as she probably sounded.

"Most girls Madame Gothel sells are put on display in groups of five. So, by the time the last girl is up for sale, she may not have good customers left. The men are given a bidding order, and those that are not as wealthy, not as polished, are put at the end. But you—you're the only girl being sold tonight. You will have a better chance at getting a decent owner."

"I don't want an owner." Azalea fisted her hands in her lap. She wanted Peter. With all of his arrogance, and sternness, and even his dreaded punishments, she wanted him.

"Well, it's not up to you," the hairdresser said, and trimmed the jaggedly cut hair. "Once we're done with this, you'll be ready."

Azalea picked at the hem of the linen dress she wore. "She's going through all this trouble with my face and hair but wants me to wear this pajama-like dress?"

The hairdresser chuckled. "You won't be wearing anything, girl. You're being sold. You'll be completely nude."

ღ ღ ღ

Azalea's entire body felt on fire. She stood at the entrance of the showroom. That's what they'd called it, a showroom. Like a car dealership! Once there, she was to remain silent and do exactly as she was told or there would be dire consequences. Or so she was told.

The hairdresser hadn't been very comforting when Azalea's tears fell. She'd slapped her naked breasts and chastised her for ruining the blush she'd applied.

Azalea had been stripped, washed, and lotioned for her showcase. Tears welled up, but she was able to keep them from falling and ruining her makeup. The hairdresser had smiled after slapping her breasts the first time—telling her the men would like to see a little blush on her tits. Azalea avoided having it done again.

"Bring her in. Gothel wants her up on the platform, under the light. Bind her hands if she resists at all." A man appeared in the doorway and gave his instructions. Apparently, the hairdresser was also to be her escort.

"I can't believe you help her sell women. What sort of person are you?" Azalea hissed when the hairdresser shoved her into movement.

"A very rich person. You girls fetch good money." With a soft pat to Azalea's bottom, she laughed.

"Ah, here she is. Azalea." Bellatrix's voice took on the persona of the doting, caring caretaker. Azalea was careful not to think of her in a maternal way. It would be too much, and she'd break down right there. She needed her wits about her for whatever was coming next.

How stupid and naive had she been! Her entire life, thinking her mother loved her so much she kept her hidden away from the horrible parts of the world. That her mother only wanted her safe. How stupid, stupid, stupid she'd been!

The room was cold. Instantly, Azalea felt her nipples tighten with increased chill. Bellatrix thought of everything. What better way to get the little bumps on her flesh and perk up her nipples, but to force the reaction with the temperature.

A bright light shone on her from her very first step into the room, blinding her from seeing anyone else. Her escort led her up a short set of stairs onto a platform and pointed to a small X marked off with tape on the floor. Azalea stood in the spot and squinted into the room. She needed to see the men. Was Peter there? Had he found out about the sale and gotten inside?

Still so naive!

"I like the tits on this one," a male voice spoke up.

"Yes, nice and round. Are they as heavy as they look?" another asked.

"You may see for yourself. One at a time, please." Bellatrix's singsong voice turned Azalea's stomach.

"And her pussy?" another rang out. "I see no hair there, very nice, but is she tight? A virgin maybe?"

"She is not a virgin, no. One man has already had his way with her, but her pussy is very tight. You may inspect her when it is your turn, though only your fingers will be allowed."

Fingers? These men were going to be allowed to probe and prod her? They were going to touch and examine? And in the end, one would buy her.

Her mind reeling, she took a step to keep from falling.

"Oh, she's quite innocent. I think the idea of all of us getting to finger that pussy of hers has made her lightheaded. Can you tie her up so she doesn't pass out?"

"Of course."

Azalea froze, looking back to the stairs. She could try to run. She had no idea of the layout of the house or where they were, but maybe she could make it out?

Before she could move, a large ring was lowered from the ceiling, and the hairdresser was there again, along with a man she didn't know. Had she really known anyone in her life? They yanked her arms up over her head.

"Don't struggle, or they'll want you punished," the hairdresser warned in a whisper. Azalea had a damn good idea what the men would want to see.

She swallowed back the cry in her throat and blinked away tears. She needed to think. There had to be a way out of this.

Her wrists were bound and hooked to the ring. The new position brought her breasts higher and stretched out her torso.

"Might as well spread those thighs for us, too," another man called out.

"Yes, bind her ankles, it will make the inspection easier anyway," Bellatrix ordered.

More cuffs were placed on her and her legs spread out past shoulder width. She was completely on display.

There was no more fighting them; the tears rolled easily.

"So pretty," one man called out. "A thousand to go first."

"Fifteen hundred," another cried.

Were they auctioning off who got to manhandle her first before the bidding began?

"Winner at three thousand. You may go up first," Bellatrix stated.

Azalea squinted, trying to see the man headed in her direction, but the light was still too bright.

She heard footsteps on the platform and turned to see him. A dark scar ran across his chin. His hair was white as snow. She closed her eyes, trying to twist away from his touch.

"If you touch her, you die," a dark voice boomed.

"What's this?" the man too close for her to ignore asked.

"If you put your old wrinkled fingers on her, I'll cut them off and feed them to you before I kill you."

Azalea opened her eyes and tried to see. She needed to see. The voice, it had to be him.

The spotlight overhead went out. Overhead lighting went on. Still, Azalea blinked, unable to see clearly.

"What the fuck is going on?" a male voice called out in the room.

At least a dozen men rose to their feet. All facing Azalea.

In the back, at the entrance to the room, three men stood, with guns drawn.

Peter stood at the forefront, his gun trained on the man standing beside Azalea.

"The auction is over," Peter stated in that low, controlled voice of his. Azalea knew what it meant, but the men in the room didn't seem to understand. No one moved.

"For your inconvenience, the women at the Annex are waiting to see to your needs tonight. Free of charge," the man to Peter's right said. He was large, not as menacing looking as Peter, but slightly taller.

"Too many rules at the Annex," one man groused.

"Then go elsewhere, but this auction is finished, and there will be no more held here. Gothel is closing," the man stated.

Peter's gun and eyes were still focused on the man on stage. Azalea needed him to look at her. She needed reassurance.

Bellatrix stepped on stage, leaving her position in the audience, shoving the old man out of the way. He stumbled then ran off, headed to the exit.

"I don't need all this fucking drama." He waved a hand in the air.

The men filed out, not giving Bellatrix or Azalea another glance. Peter still hadn't looked at her, his focus now aimed at Bellatrix.

"Get the fuck away from her," Peter demanded moving closer.

"No," Bellatrix yelled, standing behind Azalea, using her as a shield. "She's mine."

"She was never yours." The third man, the one with the short-cropped hair, moved forward, past Peter. His gun was trained on the stage.

"Oh dear." Bellatrix laughed. "Is that you, Damien?"

Who the hell was Damien?

"Look at you, all grown up. You look so much like your father with that angry expression, but still you have that witch's hair coloring, don't you?"

"Get away from Azalea." Damien came closer to the stage.

"I have my due. I'm owed," Bellatrix screeched, putting a knife to Azalea's neck.

"If you release her now, I'll let you live," Peter stated calmly, standing near Damien.

Azalea whimpered, feeling the sharp edge of the blade against her neck. Twisting away was impossible with the binds.

"Won't kill me?" Bellatrix laughed again, a high-pitched sound that sent a shiver down Azalea's body. "I've had enough of your meddling. I've had to compete with your family for too long. And now you think to take Azalea from me? Why? So you can sell her in that Annex of yours?"

"I'm not for sale." Azalea found her voice. It wasn't as loud and commanding as the men's, but she'd been able to force the words out.

"Oh? Why? You think this man loves you? You fool! Men don't love women, they use them."

"Let me go, or he will kill you." Azalea looked at Peter, focused on him even while he seemed so far away from her. Why wouldn't he look at her?

"Bellatrix, there's no way out of here," the third man spoke up, walking through the empty chairs. His gun was no longer drawn, and, in fact, he looked downright bored. "Your men have been taken care of, and the women you have locked up below now belong to Mr. Jansen."

"Hunter? Why would your uncle take my stock?"

"Because he's annoyed by you, you crazy old woman," Peter shot at her.

"You think to take Azalea home? Make her your wife? And you'll live happily ever after?" Bellatrix pushed the knife against Azalea; the bite of the edge made her wince. Peter's eyes flicked to hers for a brief moment then left her again. "So you can then toss her aside for one of the pretty whores in your stock?"

Damien moved again, stepping closer, but stilled when Azalea whimpered. The knife dug deeper, and a trickle of warm blood ran down her neck.

"Just release me. That's all you have to do," Azalea spoke again. The knife moved, more blood ran, and she clenched her teeth together.

"I don't want to hear your voice," Bellatrix ground out in her ear. She moved to her other side, still holding the knife and producing a gun.

"No!" Azalea bucked, trying to throw Bellatrix off-balance. The knife sliced across her throat, and Bellatrix stumbled.

She aimed her gun. A shot fired then another. Azalea heard a cry. Was it hers? How deep had her neck been sliced? So much blood seemed to be running down her chest. Her naked chest. So cold. The room was so damn cold.

"Peter," she cried out, unable to see through her tears. Where was he? "Peter!" she cried out again.

"Shh, I have you. It's okay, Azalea. Everything's going to be okay." Damien's voice, his hands on her wrists. "Shit! This is deep!"

She was lowered from the restraints, laid on the platform. Fabric pressed against her neck.

"It doesn't hurt." She rolled her head to the side. "Peter," she whispered.

Someone turned off the lights again. The spotlight didn't return. Voices faded.

Everything faded.

CHAPTER 24

"Peter." Ashland Titon brought him out of his haze of pain medicine and sleep.

Peter opened his eyes. "What are you doing here?" he asked his cousin and sat up in his bed.

"First of all, I live here, asshole. Second—Daniel called me."

"I told him not to do that."

"Well, he works for me, not you." Ash sank into the armchair in the corner of Peter's bedroom. "He also told me you haven't come out of this room in three days." Ash leaned forward and pressed his hands on his knees. "Just gonna lay up here and lick your wounds?"

"Shut up." Peter threw the covers back and stood up, letting his head stop spinning before heading to the bathroom to take a piss. He stubbed his toe on the hope chest and let out a curse.

"Yeah, you're going to have to watch that. Depth perception takes two eyes," Ash called after him.

Peter touched the patch over his left eye. They'd tried to save it, but there had been no hope. He was lucky to have his life; if he'd jerked in the other direction, he would have had a face full of bullet instead.

"Fuck you." Peter waved a hand at his cousin and made it to the bathroom without further incident. The pain had dulled enough not to keep him on edge, but he still needed to get used to his vision being only one-sided.

When he returned, Ash sat in the same spot, same position.

"What do you want?" Peter asked with a huff.

"I wanted to make sure for myself you were okay—and given your asshole attitude, I'd say you're fine. Physically, at least." Ash leaned back in the chair, resting his left ankle over his right knee. Obviously, settling in for a long talk.

Peter grabbed a pair of jeans from the end of the bed and stuffed his legs into them. "Well, since you can see I'm fine, why don't you be on your way?" Peter waved at the door. With Ash back, he could move into the penthouse right away. Maybe today.

"Got a call from Jansen. He'd like to know what happened to the shipment of girls he was supposed to get in exchange for getting you asshats into that auction." Ash wasn't one to mince words.

Peter snagged a T-shirt from his dresser and shoved it over his head, pushing his arms through the sleeves. "You'll have to ask Hunter that question."

"I suggested that—seeing as he's his nephew and all. Hunter's claiming there were no girls. Said the cells under Bellatrix's house were all empty." Ash tilted his head.

Peter wanted a cigarette. Strange since he hadn't lit one since high school.

"You really want to know?"

Ash shook his head. "No. I don't. But I'll choose to assume the missing girls from Bellatrix's house have nothing to do with the increase in Annex staff in the last few days."

Peter looked up at his cousin, tired and sore. "Good choice."

"And I'm sure every one of the girls we've just hired has been given a choice."

"Every last one of them. A few will be working with Daniel to find their families. But they aren't staff, they're guests." Peter sat on the edge of the bed, wanting to sink back into the softness of the mattress and try to forget the last few weeks.

"Now." Ash sighed. "The girl."

Peter closed his eye. He'd done so well at not thinking about her. Well, he'd at least been able to control the thoughts. Mostly. He'd been able to recognize he was thinking about her. That was the same thing, right?

"Her name is Azalea. Or at least that's the name Bellatrix gave her. I don't know her real name."

"Crystal. That's her real name—but from what I understand, she doesn't want to use it."

"She's doing well, then?" Peter raked a hand through his hair. He needed a shower and a damn shave.

"She's been released from the hospital. She's with her brother at Hunter's estate."

"Good." Peter nodded. His time with her hadn't been long enough. Not nearly. But he had to recognize it was time to let her go. She hadn't wanted to be there in the first place. She'd been forced, and then coerced. Better she stay with her brother and start over.

"Haven't checked your phone, then?" Ash asked.

"No. I told Daniel to get me if something came up that needed my attention. I figured a few days of quiet wouldn't hurt." Peter scratched the back of his neck.

"Well, asshole, if you had checked your phone, you would have seen that Damien and Hunter have both been trying to get ahold of you. They've demanded you see her. Apparently, when you abandon a woman, they have this silly way of expressing their pain."

Peter's eye snapped to Ash's expression. The sarcasm could be a little less dramatic, but Peter got the idea. "Is she okay?" he demanded.

"Physically? Yes. It was a pretty deep cut from what they told me, and she's going to have a nasty scar, but it's healing like it should. No damage to her throat or her vocal cords."

Peter's hands worked their way into the front pocket of his jeans. He needed to get control. His heart beat too damn fast.

"I shouldn't have let that crazy fucking woman take her out of here." Peter said the words that had been playing on repeat in his mind since the second Bellatrix pulled away from the mansion with Azalea.

"Well, it happened anyway. You can't change the past, and you sure as hell can't make her wallow it in, either." Ash stood up, his jaw set firm.

"This is different. I let her down. I told her she wouldn't be hurt."

"Fuck, Peter. You got to her in time. What were you going to do with her surrounded by four guys and Bellatrix? Just start firing into them and hope you didn't hit her, too?"

"It doesn't matter. She never wanted to be here in the first place. Now she has her freedom."

Ash shook his head. "You know, cousin, sometimes your stupidity amazes me. If you think Azalea is free because she's not here—you're a bigger idiot than I gave you credit for."

"You weren't here. You don't know."

"I know this much. I know that you are well versed in telling me when I'm in love with a woman, but fucking clueless in seeing the symptoms in yourself."

Peter clenched his jaw. In love. No, he may care about her a great deal. Because he wanted to make sure every second of every day was filled with some form of pleasure and she was always safe, didn't mean he loved her. He may think about her too often. And his chest might clench when he thought about never seeing her again, but that didn't mean he was in love.

Fuck.

Peter heaved a heavy sigh. "Even if that were true, she doesn't return the feeling."

"If you believe that, you're an idiot. Either way, get your ass over to Hunter's and see her. You owe her at least that much, don't you think?" Ash made his way toward the door.

"Since when have you gotten all touchy-feely? I think that wife of yours has ruined you," Peter shot at him.

Ash laughed. "And I'm damn grateful for it. Now get going."

Peter watched the door close behind his cousin and sat staring at the wood paneling for a long moment after. Checking in on her would be okay.

Just a quick visit.

CHAPTER 25

Azalea sat on the back porch of her brother's home, pulling the coat she'd been given tighter around her. The turtleneck sweater she wore irritated her neck, but it was better than everyone seeing the nasty wound. The stitches would come out in a few days and leave an ugly scar behind.

Forever memorializing her naivety and stupidity.

"Hey, it's getting cold out here." Damien, her brother—she had an older brother, spoke softly as he joined her on the porch. He took the seat beside her, looking out at the gardens.

"I'm warm enough," she said, still trying to get used to the idea of having family. Damien had been with her every moment at the hospital. He'd never left her bedside, and when it came time to leave, he'd taken care of everything and brought her home.

She should be more grateful. If not for Damien, she'd be on the street. Peter never had come for her.

She had waited. Once she found out the extent of his injuries, she was so relieved, she cried. He wasn't dead. He was going to be fine. And she had figured once he felt better, he'd show up.

But he never came.

She'd stopped asking about him after the second day of being home—at Damien's home. If he hadn't bothered to see her at the hospital, he wouldn't now.

Why would he? The thrill was gone. She was no longer his little mystery to solve or his toy to play with.

"I know this has been a lot for you. It's been a little weird for me, too. I remember you as a baby. I remember Mom rocking you in your room and Dad holding you while trying to play catch with me in the yard at the same time."

Damien painted a picture she wished she could remember. She never had anything like that growing up with Bellatrix. She'd suffocated her with protection—but as it turned out, it was to keep her hidden away from anyone who might recognize her and return her to her family.

"They sound perfect," she whispered.

"They were," he said.

She'd learned both of her parents had already passed away. Which was why Bellatrix had let her go out of the house now and again. Even if she was recognized, there were no parents to return her to. Her revenge had been carried out.

"I don't remember her at the house at all," Damien said with hesitation. Edging toward a conversation he'd probably been cautious about bringing up.

Azalea inhaled a long breath. "She said she loved your—I mean our father—but he refused her. I don't know how she knew him, or if she lived with us."

Damien nodded. "I'll take you to the townhouse tomorrow so you can pack anything that you want to keep."

"Thank you. What happens to all of her estates now?" Azalea asked.

"It's complicated. You see, Bellatrix Gothel doesn't really exist—not on paper, anyway, and her death—well, it also didn't really happen."

"I'm sorry to interrupt." Jaelynn, Hunter's wife opened the back door. "Azalea, you have a visitor."

"Who is it?" Damien asked in a tone with authority similar to Peter's, except Damien's came from a brotherly place.

"It's for her," Jaelynn answered, swinging the door open more to give Azalea room to walk into the house.

"Jae, who is it?" Damien asked again. The two of them seemed to enjoy biting at each other's nerves. Azalea found it endearing that they were more like brother and sister than Azalea and Damien were.

"Is it Peter?" Azalea asked.

Jaelynn smiled. "Yeah, and he looks all surly about something."

"Why would that make you smile?" Azalea asked. Out of her new family, she'd found an instant friend in Jaelynn.

"It's the same sort of surliness Hunter gets." Jaelynn leaned closer to Azalea when she walked past. "It's a good sign. Trust me." She patted her shoulder. "No. You stay away from them." Jaelynn blocked Damien when he tried to follow.

Azalea giggled. For the first time in days, and it felt good. "Just give us a few minutes, okay, Damien?"

The irritated look he flashed Jae made Azalea laugh again.

"Fine. But only a few minutes." He turned his attention to Jaelynn who remained a solid block. "Jae, if you don't get out of my way, I'm going to pick you up and take you to your room."

"Pfft. Like that scares me," Jaelynn teased.

"Then I'm going to get Hunter and tell him you were putting your nose where it doesn't belong."

That seemed to get Jaelynn's attention. Azalea noticed similarities between how Hunter spoke with Jae and how Peter addressed her. She hadn't gotten the nerve to ask about it yet, but she decided she'd need to soon.

"Bully," Jae said and stalked off. "In the front room, Azalea. Make sure you shut the door," she called over her shoulder and disappeared down the hall.

"Five minutes," Damien told Azalea. "Then I'm coming in."

"Damien." Azalea pressed a flat hand to her brother's chest. "Let me handle Peter."

"You're not alone now, Azalea," he said with his eyes softening.

"She hasn't been alone for weeks." Peter's voice set Azalea's body on edge.

"It's about damn time you showed up," Damien snapped. Giving Azalea a supportive look, he pointed at Peter. "You have five minutes." He patted Azalea's hand and headed out of the room. She and Peter were alone in the kitchen.

Turning to face him, she couldn't have been prepared to see him. A black patch covered his left eye, a stitched wound covered several inches of his left cheek. He hadn't shaved in days; black stubble covered his chin and neck. The black T-shirt clung to his muscular torso and showcased the dark-inked tattoos covering his arms.

And he was wearing jeans.

"You're wearing jeans." The thought popped out of her mouth.

Peter huffed a light laugh. "That's what you comment on? Not the pirate patch?"

"It's just you never wear jeans. You always wear slacks."

"Seems meeting you has made me start doing a lot of things I don't normally do." He moved toward her, filling the space with his presence.

She'd promised herself if he ever did show up again, she would harden herself to him. She would blow him off as easily as he'd tossed her aside. Unfortunately, the rest of her body hadn't gotten the memo. Her heart already picked up its pace, and her skin craved his touch.

"Does it hurt?" she asked, looking at the patch.

"Not anymore." He touched the edge of the patch. "Just waiting for everything to heal so I can get a glass eye."

"I don't think they're made of glass anymore." What the hell were they doing talking about his damn eye? Shouldn't she be yelling at him for abandoning her?

"Well, we'll find out," he said, taking another step and yanking the neckline of the turtleneck down to see her throat. She didn't stop him. The tiny bit of his touch on her neck felt too good to turn away. She twisted her head to give him a better view.

"It doesn't hurt so much now," she assured him when he didn't say anything.

"I will never forgive Damien for killing that witch," he muttered.

"He was protecting me."

Peter let her turtleneck go and captured her face in his palms. His dark eye met hers and locked her in place. "I wanted to kill her. I should have shot her at the house. I never should have let her take you."

Azalea wrapped her hands around his wrists, but didn't move him.

"Why did you wait to see me? I waited for you. I kept expecting you to show up, and you never did." Her voice wavered, but she pressed on. "After everything that happened, you just walked away. What are you here for?"

"You."

"Me?" She pushed his hands away and walked around the kitchen island, knowing if she didn't put something physical between them, she'd fall for his touches again. "Like you can just take me again?"

"No." He shook his head and stuffed his hands into his pockets. "I promised you'd always have a choice. And you do. I should have come to you the second I woke up. I never should have waited. I was an asshole."

She felt her jaw drop and snapped her mouth closed. "I think I've mentioned that to you before."

He grinned. "Yeah, you have. But this time, I agree. I was a complete fucking asshole for not running to your side. I thought you'd be glad to be rid of me. No more having to stay with me. With Gothel gone, and now you have a brother—I thought you would rather have him, start over without all the memories I would bring with me."

She bit down on her lower lip and remained silent for a moment. She couldn't just blurt things out as she had in the past. She needed to contain her thoughts, put them in order first.

"You idiot. I love you. Why would I want anyone but you?" Okay, she needed more practice. "You don't bring any bad memories with you. I mean—okay, maybe we met in an unconventional way—but…" How to say it, how do you tell a man you love being his—being owned and controlled, and protected by him.

"But what?" He put his hand on the island and started toward her. "Go on, finish your snit."

"You didn't do anything to me that I didn't want or didn't love. Even when you were being an asshole. Even when I couldn't sit comfortably. Every bit of it was exactly as it should be with us."

"Go on," he ordered.

"But you can't just fucking disappear on me." Her voice rose. "I needed you, Peter. When I was lying in that hospital bed trying to figure out where I fit in the world now, I needed you. Because everything I knew turned out to be a lie. I have a new brother. I have no mother. The only thing that was real—or at least what I thought was real—was you. And you turned out to be a fake, too." Tears she'd been battling for days finally fell, shaking her voice.

He was on her in an instant, pulling her against him and kissing the top of her head. She clung to him, maybe a little afraid he'd disappear again, or because she just needed to feel him close to her.

"You're right," he said after she calmed and her sobs quieted. "I should have been there. I should have let you make the call if you wanted me in your life or not. I'm sorry, sorrier than you'll know. And to make it up to you, I won't paddle your delicious ass for calling me an asshole."

She pulled back from his embrace to look at his face, not sure if he was joking or not.

"What? It's the least I can do for the woman I love."

"You—" Her protest was cut off by his lips covering hers. He kissed her with a fever that could burn her. A warning and promise of things to come. And she wanted all of it.

"Promise me," she managed to say when he released her.

"I swear it to you, Azalea, I'll never leave you again. And you don't need to figure out where you belong in this world. Because you already know."

She looked up at him, that dark, demanding glare of his and nodded. She did know.

"Say it." Bossy man.

"With you. I belong with you." She wiped a strand of hair from his forehead. "Always."

CHAPTER 26

Peter bent over the woman tied facedown to his bed, her ass a warm red, her back marked beautifully from his flogger, and her arousal glistening on her exposed pussy.

He kissed Azalea's neck, trailing more of them down her back until he got to her ass. That, he smacked with his open palm, getting the sweetest sound of pain from her.

"You've been awfully good tonight." He pulled her hips up until she managed to get to her knees. Her arms were tied to the headboard, so she wouldn't be getting far that way. He lined up his cock with her hot entrance.

"Yes, I have," she agreed. Funny how agreeable she could be when she was about to be fucked senseless.

"We'll have to make this quick. We're expected downstairs," he said, gripping her hips.

"Way to ruin the moment," she muttered, and earned another smack to her already-punished ass. She grunted, not the sort of sound that told him she was displeased.

"Quiet while I fuck you. Not a word, Azalea. I mean it. Not one fucking word." He pinched her hip to test her. A little squeal but nothing else. "Good girl. Take your fucking." He held her hips and plunged deep. Her pussy gripped him, surrounding his cock with warmth and wetness that didn't give him a fucking chance in hell to go slow with her.

Not that she would want him to.

He pulled back and plowed forward again. Another grunt.

"You like that, Azalea?" he asked and paused to see if she would answer.

She nodded.

He laughed. "Good girl." He reached forward, grabbing a fistful of her short hair and pulling her head back. "Fucking come for me, then." He fucked her hard, their bodies smacking into each other. Her groans mixed with his grunts and it took no time for them both to find their fulfillment.

Azalea screamed out his name when she found her release. He let go of her hair and rode her until he exploded inside her, filling her with his seed, marking her body again as his.

And she was. Completely his.

Peter untied her wrists, kissing the markings the rope left behind. "I love seeing these," he said, trailing his tongue over one.

"You like anything that shows others I belong to you," Azalea teased, rolling onto her back and smiling up at him.

"That's true." He dropped a kiss to her forehead. "Get dressed. Ash and Ellie are waiting on us."

Azalea sat up, wiping hair from her face. "Why would you get me all exhausted then tell me I have to spend the evening with people?" she asked.

She had a point. He probably should have waited until after they'd spent time in the club with his cousin, but when she'd stepped out of the shower with her hair messed and her body still wet, he wouldn't deny himself.

"Because I can. Now scoot." He gave her ass a quick swat to get her moving.

She grabbed the towel she'd been wearing when he'd snatched her and thrown her on the bed earlier and disappeared into her closet.

They'd been fully moved into the penthouse for almost a month. Tower was overflowing with patrons, thanks to Azalea's marketing skills, and all of her physical wounds had healed. The scar on her neck was fading slowly, and with time he hoped she'd forget it was there altogether.

"How's this?" She came out of a closet wearing a long purple dress, the V-neckline plunging down to her stomach showing some cleavage, but leaving most of her a mystery.

"I told you we don't have much time. I'll fuck you silly when we get home tonight. Stop tempting me," he joked.

She put her hands on her hips. "Seeing as a bath towel did me in a little while ago, I feel like nothing in my closet is safe."

"True enough." He buttoned his shirt and finished tucking it in before grabbing his jacket. "Okay, let's do this." He took her hand and led her to the elevator that would take them down to the club.

Ellie and Ash were already seated in their private box.

"Finally," Ash grumbled while the women hugged.

"Shut up." Peter gave him a push.

"I ordered some appetizers," Ellie said.

"Oh good. I'm starved." Azalea smiled and leaned toward Ellie. "Let's go out to lunch tomorrow. I saw a new restaurant on the lake opening up, and I want to try it."

"Of course. We'll make a day of it. I don't have any classes."

Peter watched Azalea making plans to explore the city. She couldn't get enough of seeing new places and experiencing everything she hadn't been allowed to growing up.

Peter kept a close eye, though, making sure she didn't overdo. Too much at once often made her solemn and fall quiet.

"The club is kicking ass." Ash complimented him.

"I'm thinking of opening another floor. There are plenty of them in this building not being used."

"We can have each floor be a different theme. Like one floor could be a domestic scene. Have it be a full-fledged restaurant," Azalea chimed in with her ideas.

"I love it." Ellie grinned. "What do you think, Ash?"

"Sounds like a solid idea."

"Hey, that reminds me." Ellie turned to Peter. "I couldn't find one of my black dresses when I went to get ready for tonight. I know you took a few things for Azalea—which is totally fine—but do you remember that one? It's got a low neckline—sort of how her dress is tonight?"

"Oh, yeah! I remember it," Azalea said. "He did give it to me. I'll find it and get it back to you. Sorry."

"No, no that's fine." Ellie sipped her wine.

"You can't return it," Peter interjected.

"Why not?" Azalea asked.

Peter looked at her, enjoying the innocence of her expression at the moment. "Because it ripped when I tore it off you."

The blush was quick to appear and raged hard on her cheeks. Ash burst out laughing.

"Peter," Azalea chastised, looking mortified. "I'm so sorry, Ellie."

"It's fine. Really." Ellie smiled, glancing at Ash. "It happens in this family."

Peter picked up Azalea's hand. "You have two families. You have Damien—and you have us." He pressed a kiss to her knuckles. "You could not be more loved, Azalea." He dropped a kiss on her forehead.

His chest warmed. Taking the small box out of his pocket, he opened it and pulled out the ring he'd been hiding. "You were right. I love anything that marks you as mine." He held the ring out to her. "Be my wife?"

"You're asking?" Azalea searched his expression. He'd promised she'd always have a choice.

"It's really more symbolic—but yes, I'm asking." He grinned.

"Of course, I will." She kissed him. He slid the ring, a silver band with a lilac stone surrounded by diamonds, onto her finger.

"Well, another Titon bites the dust." Ash lifted his glass in a toast.

"Okay, we've socialized enough. Let's go." Peter stood up and grabbed her hand.

"We just got here," Azalea pointed out, laughing while he pulled her from her seat.

"Ash and Ellie understand," he assured her, giving Ash a nod and Ellie a wink—enjoying her blush almost as much as Azalea's.

Peter led her back to the elevator and pressed the code for the penthouse.

Azalea held his hand tight. "You've given me everything, Peter."

He pushed her against the glass wall and kissed her. "You are everything, Azalea."

The elevator doors slid open, and remained that way until Peter finished kissing his fiancée.

"Three seconds to get out of this dress before I rip it off," he ordered and gave her ass a resounding smack.

"Good thing, I saved time and didn't wear any panties."

He laughed. "You don't have any to wear." He loved controlling the use of her panties. Kept them in his drawer and doled them out when absolutely needed.

"I love you, Peter Titon." She wrapped her arms around his neck.

"And I love you." He kissed her. "One, two, three," he rattled off the numbers and grabbed hold of her neckline.

And they lived mostly happily ever after…

ღ ღ ღ

THANK YOU FOR READING TOWER! I hope you love Peter and Azalea's story! They'd love to meet all of the people, so please, spread the word- tell a friend about these books!

Want more dark romance from Measha Stone? Subscribe to Measha Stone's Newsletter http://bit.ly/2tTBRmV

You're not going to want to miss out on reading Measha's #1 Best Seller in Gothic Romance, BEAST. Ellie makes Ash an offer he can't refuse, but he plans to take even more. Like everything!

Don't miss Measha Stone's Owned and Protected Series, starting with Protecting His Pet. It's chalked full of dark romance and pet play!

Please join Measha in her Facebook Group, Measha's Madhouse for exclusive giveaways and sneak peeks of future books. You can join here: https://bit.ly/2M9C9Op

Amazon http://amzn.to/2BPnQd3
Book Bub http://bit.ly/2DUs0hY
Facebook https://bit.ly/2kzQT7r

ALSO BY MEASHA STONE

EVER AFTER
Beast

OWNED AND PROTECTED
Protecting His Pet
Protecting His Runaway
His Captive Pet
His Captive Kitten

BLACK LIGHT SERIES
Black Light Valentine Roulette
Black Light Cuffed
Black Light Roulette Redux
Black Light Suspicion

WINDY CITY
Hidden Heart
Secured Heart
Indebted Heart
Liberated Heart